Envy

Also from Rachel Van Dyken

Liars, Inc.
Dirty Exes

The Players Game Series
Fraternize
Infraction

The Consequence Series
The Consequence of Loving Colton
The Consequence of Revenge
The Consequence of Seduction
The Consequence of Rejection

The Wingmen Inc. Series
The Matchmaker's Playbook
The Matchmaker's Replacement

Curious Liaisons Series
Cheater
Cheater's Regret

The Bet Series
The Bet
The Wager
The Dare

The Ruin Series
Ruin
Toxic
Fearless
Shame

The Eagle Elite Series
Elite
Elect
Enamor
Entice
Elicit
Bang Bang
Enforce
Ember
Elude
Empire
Enrage
Eulogy
Envy

Envy

An Eagle Elite Novella

By Rachel Van Dyken

1001 Dark Nights

EVIL EYE

CONCEPTS

Envy
An Eagle Elite Novella
By Rachel Van Dyken

1001 Dark Nights

Copyright 2018 Rachel Van Dyken
ISBN: 978-1-948050-27-2

Foreword: Copyright 2014 M. J. Rose

Published by Evil Eye Concepts, Incorporated

Acknowledgments from the Author

I thank God every day for the opportunity to create stories and do what I love. Thank you so much to my husband and son for putting up with me. Readers, you will never fully understand how much I appreciate you. Without you I wouldn't have a job, not only that, without you it wouldn't be as fun as it is. I love gushing about books with you guys and I'm so blessed to be part of this amazing reading community. A huge special thanks to Molly McAdams for letting me hijack her Borello family (The Rebel Series https://www.mollysmcadams.com/rebel-series) and using them as a special cameo in Vic's book. It made the book that much better and more exciting for readers, which is always what we aim to do as authors! Be sure to check out her series. Thank you, readers, for being you. Bloggers thank you for constantly pushing books. And to Liz for taking a chance on me, haha. Thank you for inviting me into the 1001 Dark Nights family, it's not just a pleasure it's an honor to write for you guys. I hope everyone enjoys Envy! And if you want a super fun safe place to talk books, don't forget to join Rachel's New Rockin Readers on Facebook! Blood in. No Out. HUGS, RVD

Sign up for the 1001 Dark Nights Newsletter
and be entered to win a Tiffany Key necklace.

There's a contest every month!

Go to www.1001DarkNights.com to subscribe.

**As a bonus, all subscribers can download
FIVE FREE exclusive books!**

One Thousand and One Dark Nights

Once upon a time, in the future...

*I was a student fascinated with stories and learning.
I studied philosophy, poetry, history, the occult, and
the art and science of love and magic. I had a vast
library at my father's home and collected thousands
of volumes of fantastic tales.*

*I learned all about ancient races and bygone
times. About myths and legends and dreams of all
people through the millennium. And the more I read
the stronger my imagination grew until I discovered
that I was able to travel into the stories... to actually
become part of them.*

*I wish I could say that I listened to my teacher
and respected my gift, as I ought to have. If I had, I
would not be telling you this tale now.
But I was foolhardy and confused, showing off
with bravery.*

*One afternoon, curious about the myth of the
Arabian Nights, I traveled back to ancient Persia to
see for myself if it was true that every day Shahryar
(Persian: شهريار, "king") married a new virgin, and then
sent yesterday's wife to be beheaded. It was written
and I had read, that by the time he met Scheherazade,
the vizier's daughter, he'd killed one thousand
women.*

Something went wrong with my efforts. I arrived in the midst of the story and somehow exchanged places with Scheherazade — a phenomena that had never occurred before and that still to this day, I cannot explain.

Now I am trapped in that ancient past. I have taken on Scheherazade's life and the only way I can protect myself and stay alive is to do what she did to protect herself and stay alive.

Every night the King calls for me and listens as I spin tales. And when the evening ends and dawn breaks, I stop at a point that leaves him breathless and yearning for more. And so the King spares my life for one more day, so that he might hear the rest of my dark tale.

As soon as I finish a story... I begin a new one... like the one that you, dear reader, have before you now.

Chapter One

Renee

"Gotcha!" I grabbed Serena's chubby foot and pretended to shove it in my mouth. She squealed and pulled it away, only to put it back again with a giggle. Babies. I shook my head and did it repeatedly for the next twenty minutes, causing hiccups of laughter. She was only eighteen months but the cutest baby I'd ever seen, next to the little guy currently trying to stack blocks on Serena's right. I called him Junior since he had his dad Phoenix's same name.

Nixon, the boss to the Abandonato family, walked by and winked at his little one, careful to hide his Glock in the back of his jeans as he bent over and kissed her on the head.

I looked away.

I never stared too long.

Fact: My parents specifically told me not to speak to any of the bosses unless spoken to.

To drive their point home, they told me a story about one of the made men interrupting family dinner and getting shot in the kneecaps.

They let him bleed on the floor for an hour before finally helping him—the guy still walks with a limp to this day. I wish I could say they were scary stories you told your kids to put the fear of God in them, something you and your siblings whisper about late at night.

But I knew it was true. All of it.

The mafia was a very real beast.

And it took no prisoners.

It would rather kill them.

With a sigh, I kept playing with Serena and tried to make myself small. I didn't need the attention, and while Nixon had always been nothing but kind to me, I knew what he was capable of.

Phoenix Nicolasi walked into the room next—no, he commanded the room, the very air that dared touch his skin—he wielded it with his silence.

Terrifying…did not adequately describe him. And the fact that he had black folders, one for every single person connected to the family, including the cappo—our version of the Godfather if you want to get specific—well, it was petrifying.

I had friends from college that complained about working at coffee shops or in the mall during the summer. I lied and said I worked at a doctor's office.

Phoenix pulled out his gun and checked to make sure it was loaded.

Yeah. Not quite a place that saved lives and cured runny noses.

Serena tugged on my hair to get my attention. It was like she could sense my fear, the way that my body carried a slight tremble whenever the men were near me and the women weren't in the same room.

It was normal behavior for those guys.

To bust out their weapons at any point without thinking about the little eyes that watched, that wanted to be just like Dad, killer and all.

I tried not to judge.

It was hard.

They were mafia bosses—I got it.

Or at least I thought I understood it since I had grown up around it. But my upbringing wasn't as severe. My dad was a Nicolasi and always kept things quiet around us. It wasn't until I was twelve that I realized it wasn't normal for us to make as much money as we did through two jewelry stores and five laundromats.

I wrongly assumed that every business owner with a lot of cash drove a bulletproof Mercedes to protect their family. The older I got, the more horrified I became of the life my father lived, the life he forced us to live, and the complete unrest I felt every time I closed my eyes and prayed for him to come home.

He was a made man.

One of the best in the family, which meant Phoenix trusted him, which in turn meant he trusted me to watch his little boy. And every time Phoenix looked at his phone I wondered if it was my dad texting, if he was alive, if he was okay. He'd been gone for a month. We hadn't heard from him except for a few *"hey, I'm alive"* texts.

I hated this life.

And I wanted out.

"Renee." Nixon leaned down and touched my shoulder. "Are you okay?"

I stilled.

Remembered not to look directly into his eyes and forced a smile. "I'm just tired, you know how it is."

"Kids do that to a person," Phoenix piped in, finally sheathing the knives he'd apparently pulled out in the last few seconds that I'd been thinking about my dad. "We need to leave in five."

Nixon stood.

I looked away.

I had to.

It made me sick to my stomach the blood these men had on their hands and the way they so casually talked about killing as if they were discussing the latest episode of *This Is Us*.

I forced a smile at Serena and Junior just as the front door swung open, nearly coming off its hinges.

There he stood.

My nightmare.

Vic Corazon Abandonato.

In all his gory glory.

Tight black pants.

Tight black shirt.

Enough guns strapped to him to win an all-out war.

And no smile.

The man never smiled. It wasn't in his makeup to smile. The one time he smiled was at Chase, and I think it was just a happy accident because Chase looked as shocked as the rest of the group did. I glanced away, again making sure I wasn't drawing attention to myself, and fed the kids.

Vic was a silent killer. I imagined that people didn't even know they were dying until they saw the blood running like a river from their chests.

I shivered.

That's what assassins for the mafia did. They weren't made men, they weren't in line for boss. They did the dirty work-and they took the fall for it. They had one job. Protect the family at all costs.

He was the exact opposite of what I wanted for my life. He wasn't the happily ever after.

I suddenly couldn't wait to leave for school the following week. I was studying journalism at Brown, and even though I was going to be leaving the kids behind, I was ready to leave all of this behind too.

Freedom. Finally.

The death, the blood, the stares from Vic when he thought I wasn't looking.

I self-consciously tucked my cropped black hair behind my ears and stood, picking up both kids and carrying them out of the room just as Nixon laughed and said, "You scared her away."

Vic's smooth, arrogant voice fired back. "It's what I do best. Scare people."

Seconds later I walked back into the room to grab one of the discarded toys Serena needed. I didn't miss the way his eyes locked on me before he gave me his back. I exhaled the breath I'd been holding with a shudder and moved the kids as far away from the devil as I could.

If only I could save them.

Protect their innocence for more than one summer.

And keep the darkness at bay just a little bit longer.

Chapter Two

Vic

She made it impossible not to stare, with her luscious pink lips and hooded brown-eyed gaze, almost like she was Sleeping Beauty waking up from a long, much-needed nap. It hurt like hell knowing that a woman like that would never look twice at a man like me.

A foot soldier.

Killer.

Demon.

I had no heart or soul to give her—I'd already sworn it to the families. Besides, what use did I have for fairytales?

"You're scarier looking than usual." Nixon piped up from the back seat, smug expression firmly in place. Between the ink on both arms, chest, and the lip piercing, he looked anything but a mob boss. More like a motorcycle gang leader who'd gotten lost in the Chicago suburbs.

Phoenix cracked a rare smile while I kept my eyes locked on the road ahead of me, on the task at hand. I pulled up to Chase's house and waited.

When he didn't show after five minutes, Phoenix leaned over the console and honked the horn.

Bringing attention to us.

To me.

I scowled and quickly checked the perimeter.

Behind us all clear.

Next to us clear.

No cars in sight.

I exhaled in relief. "Boss, I would really appreciate you not letting everyone know our location."

Phoenix shrugged. "I'd like to see someone try to kill the three of us, on the street we own, in the city we command."

A throbbing headache pulsed behind my eyes. "And yet, they do, on a daily fucking basis."

"Language." Nixon piped up from the backseat, waving his gun in the air.

We'd been trying to cut back on account of the kids.

I'd already lost a solid fifty dollars to that damn swear jar, and I barely spoke! Nixon said it was because whenever I did speak it was inappropriate for small ears.

I inwardly rolled my eyes just as the front door opened. Chase's wide stride ate up the distance as he finally made his way to the SUV and got in.

"Sorry." He slammed the door behind him.

It was quiet.

Too quiet.

With a frown I finally looked to Phoenix, whose eyebrows were raised to his hairline.

Nixon was biting down on his lip with a smirk. "You, ah, you forgot a spot."

Chase frowned and then touched his mouth with the back of his hand and wiped off a smear of red lipstick. His voice took on a threatening tone. "Not another word."

Nixon held up his hands.

I chuckled.

Gaining everyone's attention.

"What?" Chase kicked my seat. "Out with it."

"Shirt's on backwards," I said as I pulled out onto the street to the guys' howls of laughter and two middle fingers directed at the rearview mirror. "And it's inside out."

"I knew that," he grumbled, peeling off his shirt and flipping it right-side out. "I was just in a hurry…"

"Bullshit." Phoenix coughed.

"Like I can't hear you," Chase growled.

"You know, it's okay to have sex with your new wife. Nobody's going to judge you for that," Nixon said quietly.

The tension in the car was so thick I almost jumped out my side and let them fend for themselves.

Chase's first wife had betrayed the families.

He had just gotten married again.

She was pregnant.

And things were tense.

Tense because he didn't trust anyone anymore.

Tense because he kept losing his soul with each De Lange kill.

Tense because we were in a war that I often wondered if we could win, especially with the De Lange family trying to constantly pick a fight. They had nothing left to lose.

Which meant they were a dangerous foe.

And since Chase had been nominated as their keeper until we could get them under the four remaining families' control—that meant he was bloodthirsty and still dealing with a bit of guilt over how his new wife had nearly died just to save him.

It was a clusterfuck of drama that would keep a sane person awake at night.

I stayed out of it.

I stayed out of all of it.

It was a lonely existence.

Which made me always circle back to Renee.

Beautiful. Innocent. Renee.

Every time I saw her I wanted to yell at her to run. To escape this place and never come back. I'd seen the toll it took on the bosses' wives. This was no place for a wide-eyed innocent college student who played nanny during the summers.

I gripped the steering wheel so hard my fingers turned white.

"What's wrong with Vic?" Chase's voice cut through the tense silence. "He's quieter than usual. Hey, big guy, you pissed I flipped you off?"

"You flip him off every day," Phoenix pointed out.

"He's always quiet."

"You know what would be great?" Chase grinned menacingly into the rearview mirror.

I didn't like where this was going. Months ago, I had basically been his babysitter—*make sure he doesn't kill himself or anyone else without permission.* And he said he'd get even for cockblocking him early on with Luciana, his wife.

The worst he could do was kill me.

I'd probably welcome the peace.

"What?" I finally asked, taking the next turn and hitting the accelerator. "What would be great, Chase?"

"If you—" He pointed his knife at me, tapping me on the shoulder. "—got laid."

"Here we go," Phoenix said under his breath.

"I'm serious. He's almost as fun to be around as I used to be, and that's not just sad, that's bordering on pathetic. You need an orgasm." I rolled my eyes as a growl escaped my lips. "Or…ten."

A prickling sensation ran down my spine as Nixon cut in. "You know he can't—"

"—We're almost there, cut the small talk," Phoenix barked.

I turned the next corner and pulled up to the warehouse.

It was the perfect setup for what we had to do.

Dante and Sergio were already there with Tex, the cappo. And if things went smoothly, Frank, one of the older, retired bosses, would be there too.

He played the good cop since none of us really knew how to do that.

We were bad. Through and through.

After I parked, I got out of the SUV first, followed by the guys. Every move we made carried the potential for a deadly change in circumstances. I held up my hand for them to stop and opened the warehouse door ahead of them, pointing my gun into the darkness beyond, tensed and waiting for gunshots.

I always prepared for the worst.

Body bags.

Death.

Cover ups.

Dante, the Alfero boss, poked his head around the corner and sighed. "They finally gave you a gun?"

"Shut the hell up." I shoved past him. "I could have shot you."

"Eh, bet you'd miss."

I rolled my eyes. Little shit drove me to drink on a daily basis. Literally.

"You guys finally made it to the party, huh?" Dante crossed his arms and led the way across the cement floor and into the next section of the warehouse. The section that was soundproof, for obvious reasons.

A man was hanging from the ceiling by his hands next to two others sitting in chairs, their hands tied behind their backs. A gag was in each of their mouths and blood caked their cheeks like a bright blush.

Frank was standing in the corner with a cigar in his mouth. His scarf wrapped tightly around his neck, and his black fedora—always a hat with that guy—perched on his head like he was on his way to fashion week and decided to stop and dirty himself up a bit.

Tex had his sleeves rolled up and was slowly loading his gun, taking time with each bullet while the hostages watched. And Sergio was standing next to him with a needle in his gloved hands, always ready to inject some sort of concoction that helped people talk.

"See?" Dante shrugged. "Party."

"Looks like you have things…handled." Phoenix stepped around me and pulled out one of his knives, then held it out in front of him. "Which one wants to go first?"

Nobody said a word.

"Hmm." Phoenix shrugged. "Guess it's ladies' choice…Chase?"

Fuck you, Chase mouthed before walking over to them. His eyes roamed over their faces like he was memorizing their fear to use against them later; or maybe he was just saving it for himself so he could feed off of it late at night when he needed energy.

"You." Chase nodded to the guy hanging from his hands. "You look…petrified."

The man didn't flinch.

"Fear, it has a certain smell… To some it smells like death, but to men like us? You may as well have given us a shot of adrenaline and added a line of cocaine for kicks… Your fear makes it harder on you. Keep your secrets and die. Keep your secrets and suffer. Those are your choices. Blink once if you want to die." The man started blinking violently.

Chase smirked. "That's what I thought. So here's what's going to happen. You're going to tell me everything you know about who's currently leading the De Lange family, who's suddenly decided to start helping finance them and make a war between us—and then Vic here is going to beat you until you lose the ability to ever speak again." He lowered his voice. "Aren't I merciful?"

"A regular fuckin' saint." Tex chuckled as he kicked a chair toward the guy's feet. He stood by while Chase sliced the rope with his knife.

And when the guy sat on the chair, and the gag was pulled, the first thing the idiot did was spit in Chase's face.

I lunged, ready to force the respect out of him.

Chase held up his hand.

I hated that feeling. The feeling that I needed permission to end someone when they deserved it.

This guy deserved it.

"Something on your mind?" Chase sneered.

"How's your new wife?" he countered with a bloody grin; he was already missing two front teeth and his nose looked broken.

The tension in the room skyrocketed. The De Langes had not only tried to kill Chase's current wife—they were also the same blood line of his dead wife, the one who'd betrayed the families. Suffice to say, nobody really wanted the De Langes alive, and if you wanted to stay alive, you'd best not mention Chase's wife to anyone.

"Alive." Chase's voice snapped, causing the tension to thicken even more. "Which is more than I can say about you." He backed away slowly. "Have fun, Vic...not too much though. Leave some for the rest of us." He gave me a simple nod. A nod full of respect, full of justice, vengeance. We did not allow rats to live. And I would kill anyone who threatened my family. It was my vow. My curse.

"I don't like sharing," I growled as I moved toward the chair and locked eyes with the next man on the list of men I'd been ordered to kill.

Tunnel vision.

Darkness.

My demons came out to play.

I smiled.

While he screamed.

Chapter Three

Renee

"The kids are asleep." I yawned behind my hand while Trace motioned for me to follow her down the hall. It had been a long day.

My feet hurt.

Note to self: Don't wear new shoes to work when you have kids who run to each new activity like it's a race. I'd never wanted a massage so bad.

"Thank you." She had dark circles under her eyes and wasn't wearing much makeup, which wasn't typical of any of the wives. They always looked put together, fierce, expensive, almost like it was part of a uniform. Though if any of them just went natural it would probably be Trace more than the others.

"Hey." I touched her arm without thinking about it, then snatched my hand back. "Are you okay?"

She stared past me like she wasn't really there in the kitchen with me. "I just...I hate it when they're late, you know?"

"The bosses?"

"All of them." She shrugged. "Ever since..." She looked down at the ground. "When you lose one person, it kinda makes you worried you're going to somehow lose them all. I know it sounds stupid and morbid, but it just wears on you, and when you're fighting a stupid cold it doesn't help."

I scrunched up my nose. "The cold I can help with. The death. Well, I can only hope and pray that they come home safe."

"Thank you." She pulled me in for a hug.

I stiffened, then returned it. "For what?"

"For listening. I try not to burden the other girls. They have enough to worry about without me falling apart."

I pulled away. "Being strong sucks, but somebody has to do it."

"I know." She smiled. "So what about the cold, what's your secret?"

"Ah." I went in search of a coffee mug and then went over to the liquor cabinet and poured two shots of whiskey. "Do you have any lemons?"

"In the fridge."

"Great."

I grabbed the tea kettle that had been on from the drink I'd made earlier and poured the still hot water into the cup then added the splash of lemon from the fridge. I knew the honey was in the pantry because I'd added it to some toast that morning.

"Here you go!" I handed the drink over. "Old family trick. Helps with sore throats, but it also makes you sleepy."

"Sleep." She closed her eyes and let out a little moan. "Sounds amazing."

"I leave for a few hours and you're making my wife moan?" Nixon smiled as he walked into the room. His face was tight. His hands didn't have blood on them, but I imagined that at one point tonight, they had.

They all had blood on their hands—always would.

I inspected his clothes like it would make me feel better.

It didn't.

Because they weren't the same clothes he'd left in, meaning he'd changed so he wouldn't come home with blood speckles all over his shirt.

"It's this stupid cold." Trace looked ready to stomp her foot. "Sorry, I kept her late tonight so I could try to power through."

Nixon bent down and captured her mouth in a searing kiss that had me averting my eyes and looking out the window awkwardly just in time to see Phoenix walk in. He was paranoid about someone kidnapping Junior and hurting Bee whenever he was gone, so they stayed the night at Nixon's fortress whenever business was serious.

"Renee?" Nixon called, startling me.

I jerked back around, forgetting not to make eye contact. His icy gaze locked on me, intense, beautiful. Then again, they were all good looking—it should be a crime for killers to look like super models.

He sucked in his lip ring and crossed his arms. "Did you hear anything I just said?"

Heat spread across my cheeks. *Please don't kill me.* "No, I'm so sorry, it won't happen again, I was just...I'm tired."

His eyebrows drew together in concern. "I know, that's why I don't want you driving. Plus..." He looked back at Trace. "It's not safe. In fact, I wanted to talk to you about something..."

My skin started to itch all over.

"...but it can wait until you've slept a few hours." His smile was warm. I couldn't read him. I'd nannied for them for a few months, and he'd never really smiled at me, at least from what I could remember. Maybe Trace helped make him more human. "I'm going to have Vic take you home."

My ears started to ring.

Anyone but Vic.

He was too intense. He rarely spoke. I couldn't read him and got constant anxiety around him—It didn't help that I'd never once seen him without a sneer on his face like he was pissed off at the world and was hellbent on destroying it.

Heck, I would take Phoenix and I'm pretty sure he dreams of killing in his sleep, with a smile on his face and death as his own personal lullaby.

Vic chose the perfect moment to walk in. He turned his head slightly toward our conversation, kept walking, then tripped.

"Shit! Damn it. What the hell!" he roared.

I jumped when his hand thrust a race car in the air.

Whoops.

"Curse jar!" Trace laughed.

Vic stood to his feet and slammed the car onto the table, leveling me with a glare in the process, then reached into his pocket and pulled out a twenty.

"It's only five dollars per curse word," Nixon pointed out.

Vic held up his hand. "Who left the damn car on the floor?"

"Ah, and now you're at twenty. Got it." Nixon's laughter joined Trace's.

"Um, it was probably me. I thought I cleaned up but...I must have missed one." My voice sounded weak. I felt stupid.

Vic's face actually softened. "Should have watched where I was going."

"That's as close to an apology as you'll get." Trace nodded to me. "Vic, take her home? Please?"

His face visibly paled.

Seriously?

At the thought of what? Being alone in a car with me?

Fantastic.

He looked ready to puke.

Nothing like feeling wanted.

I mean, if a murderer can't even sit next to me, what hope did I have for marriage? Good thing I had an on-again-off-again boyfriend that liked me enough to kiss me and see me naked.

Though it had been weeks.

Months.

Who was I kidding? I hadn't heard from him all summer.

"What about you?" Vic pointed between Trace and Nixon.

"We have security, we're fine. Just keep her safe and check the house, all right?" He grabbed Trace's hand, kissed it, and led her out of the kitchen.

I gulped and stared at Vic.

He stared right back.

His eyes reminded me of Nixon's, too pretty for a man, unfair that his eyelashes were long too. His face was all hard angry lines, his jaw had absolutely no fat on it, and I truly wasn't sure if he had his teeth anymore, on account of the fact that he didn't smile.

His eyes locked on mine. "Should we go?"

"Yeah." I tried to keep the shaking out of my voice as I walked through the kitchen, grabbed my purse from the table, and stood next to him.

He didn't budge.

"Um?" I pointed to the door.

Which made him smirk.

And made my jaw nearly detach from my face.

That smirk.

It shouldn't be sexy.

It had no right to be sexy.

Straight white teeth.

Dimples.

The man had dimples!

Who knew?

"I walk behind you, always behind you. If I walk in front of you, I can't protect you. And that's my job." It was the most he'd ever spoken to me.

I nodded dumbly and walked ahead of him, feeling a slight touch of his fingertips on my lower back as he steered me to the garage.

Toward his G-Wagon.

It wasn't just that he was paid well.

He was an Abandonato.

The guy could shit money every day of his life and still have enough to buy a small country and outrun the FBI.

He could do it ten times over. That's what happens when you're mafia royalty.

I could feel the pulse of his body heat through his fingertips on my back as he reached around me and opened the door.

I crawled in, dropping my purse at my feet, and was ready to slam the door when he ducked his massive body in and buckled my seatbelt for me—and pulled to make sure it was connected.

"You good?" he asked in a soft voice.

I gaped and then mutely nodded my head.

The door clicked shut.

I shivered.

I wasn't cold.

It was the way he'd stared at me.

It was every brush of his fingertips.

Yeah, I must be really tired.

I gave my head a shake when he got in the driver's side and his cologne floated toward my face. He smelled rich. Expensive. The mixture of leather and spice danced around my nose as he started the engine.

And then his hands were by me as he hit the seat warmers, clearly mistaking my shivering for being cold. He turned on the heat and directed it toward me, all before he even put on his seatbelt.

"Do you want a water?" he asked, casually pulling out of the garage and through the security gates.

"Um…" I licked my lips. "Sure."

He stopped the car.

Unbuckled his seat belt and reached behind him. Then handed me a cold bottle, only to get buckled again and take the car out of park.

Stunned, I held the cold water and stared at him. "You could have done that without stopping the car or unbuckling your seatbelt."

"Yes."

"So? Why waste the time?"

"We're outside the gates of Nixon's house. Anyone could be out here waiting. We have enemies coming at us from all sides. I refuse to take any chances. All it takes is for me to hesitate. It takes one second. One second where I'm not paying attention. I would regret that one second for the rest of my life; it would hang over my head. I wouldn't wish that guilt on anyone, I have enough deaths to pay for—I would not survive having yours on my head too."

"Because you would get killed?" I croaked.

That smirk, that beautiful smirk, crept across his face again. "No, Renee, because I wouldn't want to live—not knowing that I was allowed to and you were in the cold, hard ground."

I started to sweat.

My body was overheating at his words. He acted like he cared. He acted like I mattered. It didn't make sense. I was a nobody. My dad was high up in the ranks, sure, but I was his daughter.

A college student.

A nanny.

Why would Vic even care?

I chewed on that thought the entire drive to our house.

The lights were low since my mom and aunt had decided to go away for the weekend—which they did often when my dad wasn't home. It took her mind off his potential death. Lucky her.

Vic reached across the consul and grabbed my arm. "Why is the house so dark?"

I shrugged. "My mom's gone, it's just me for the next few days."

"No." He unbuckled his seatbelt.

I let out a humorous laugh. "Uh yeah, they're gone. Look, it's fine, I stay by myself all the time. I'm twenty-one." I was ready to graduate this year! "Plus I know how to shoot a gun—and I'm not a target, believe me."

He shook his head. "I'm calling Nixon."

"You're not calling Nixon. It's seriously fine, don't bother him with—"

He was already tapping like a maniac on his phone.

It filtered into the car on speaker.

"Everything okay?"

"She's alone. The house is dark."

"Shit."

I threw my hands into the air. They were all overreacting.

"Exactly." Vic looked at me out of the corner of his eye, his expression almost smug. "What do you want me to do?"

"You can't stay with her alone."

Vic rolled his eyes. "Because I can't take care of her?"

"Because her father would kill me if he knew I left his only daughter with one of the cousins who used to sleep his way through most of Eagle Elite University—didn't you screw a professor?"

Vic winced. "Yeah, you're on...speaker."

Silence and then, "I know."

"Bastard."

"That's another five for the swear jar."

"Bastard isn't a swear word!" Vic roared. "And you just said shit!"

I hid a laugh behind my hand.

He turned to me, eyes wide. "Tell him!"

I held my hands up in the air. "Oh, I'm not taking sides, too dangerous, and I like living, but if I were to take sides...always choose the boss."

Nixon cackled. "Her dad raised her right."

Vic swore again.

"That's ten." Nixon laughed harder.

"Back to the topic at hand." Vic rubbed his eyes, and it was the first time I really saw a crack in his inhuman ability to look bored at everyone and everything. Instead, he just looked tired. Join the club, right? "What do you want me to do?"

"Bring her back here, she can stay with us."

Ah, recurring nightmare, we meet again!

"Nixon," I piped up, a bit desperate. "I swear I'm safe. Nobody would try anything and—"

"Are you arguing with me?" He sounded surprised.

"No, I just..." My eyes pleaded with Vic.

"One night." Nixon sighed. "Vic will stay with you one night. Not a word to your father, I don't want to have to shoot one of Phoenix's best men because he gets pissed at me...and Vic, try to keep your hands to yourself."

"I'm a changed man, you know that." Vic sounded sad, his entire body braced like he was waiting for a bomb to drop on him.

Nixon waited a few beats then uttered, "I know, man. I know."

"We'll see you in the morning." Vic hit the end button and cut the engine. "Looks like you're stuck with me for another twelve hours."

"Hah." I saw absolutely no humor in the situation. It was the lesser of two evils. It was just Vic, just terrifying, silent, brooding, sexy Vic. What could possibly go wrong in twelve hours?

Chapter Four

Vic

I would have been fine.

Completely fine.

Had Nixon not brought up my past. On. Purpose.

I wasn't stupid.

He wasn't stupid.

Which meant he had a reason to warn her.

Which meant I was a fucking idiot for thinking that I had hidden all the stolen glances I'd sent her way.

I cringed just thinking about it.

If Nixon knew, that meant the other guys did too.

Which also meant they were probably taking bets behind my back to see how long I would last before I snapped and tried kissing her.

I licked my suddenly dry lips as I followed her into the house, my eyes taking in every inch of brick, every speck of dust, every shadow that lurked from the trees.

I held my gun out and ready while she unlocked the door. The house appeared newer, it was two stories of Nicolasi money—hell, the walls were built on blood. I wondered how many souls were taken in order to pay for this house—how many lives changed through its existence.

"See?" Renee spread her arms wide and gave a little shrug. The moonlight cast a glow through the impressive kitchen window, giving her such an ethereal look I stopped breathing for a second before schooling my features. "Nothing to worry about, nobody here to kill me."

I didn't relax my stance or lower my gun. "So you checked the crawl spaces? Closets? Dark corners?" I took a step as she shook her head slowly. "Then surely you checked the pantry, right? I mean it's right behind you. Hell, there could be someone with a gun trained on that pretty mop of hair right now and you wouldn't know until it was too late." Her eyes widened like she hadn't thought of it. Of course she hadn't. It wasn't her job to think about the monsters in the dark, just like it wasn't her job to protect herself. That was why she had me.

I reached behind her and opened the pantry, pointing my gun inside before shutting the door and facing her again. "It's clear."

Her lower lip trembled. "I didn't think of the pantry."

"It's not your job to obsess over the pantry," I whispered in a gruff voice. "It's your job to listen to me when I'm trying to do my best to keep you safe."

She looked away. "Can't save everyone."

"But there's absolutely nothing wrong with trying, Renee."

I said her name.

It tasted sweet on my tongue.

The moan that wanted to follow was barely suppressed by clenching my teeth together.

"Are you going to do a sweep of the house?" she asked quietly.

"Did you want to join me?"

"Am I safer with you or by myself in the kitchen?"

"With me," I lied. Physically she would always be safe from our enemies—but I knew the truth in my soul. I was just as dangerous to her as a bullet. My being with her would eventually kill her.

All the wives knew it.

They knew that eventually there would be blood.

And if their husbands were gone—it was only a matter of time before it was theirs that was spilled.

I'd like to think that's why we drank wine like water.

Because when you constantly stare down your impending doom, you start wanting to celebrate every extra minute you've been given.

"Let's go." I nodded toward the hall. My footsteps whispered against the carpet. Nothing seemed out of place—which was almost more suspicious. People were messy. The hallways were lined with family pictures of Renee smiling with her parents. A heaviness settled on my shoulders.

"She can't know," Phoenix had said earlier that night. "At least not yet."

I knew she was close with her parents. I also knew that they were dishonest with her. And she wondered why she was the one nannying the kids.

Why she was constantly under the watchful eye of Nixon.

I shook my head and kept walking with a stiff Renee next to me.

I cleared each room, each closet, each corner, and twenty minutes later when I felt it was safe enough for her to do more than breathe at my side, I lowered my gun and put it back in its holster.

"All good?" Renee stepped away. She rarely looked me in the eyes, but this time they locked onto me for a good three seconds before she tucked her hair behind her ear and walked farther and farther away.

I almost reached out and grabbed her arm.

Almost jerked her against my chest.

Almost confessed it all.

The lies they'd told.

The secrets we kept.

All to keep her safe.

All to keep her in the dark.

To keep her alive.

"All good," I rasped.

She bit down on her lower lip then sucked it between her teeth before almost disappearing down the hall.

Did she expect me to follow her?

"Hey," she called. "You coming? Or do you not plan on sleeping tonight?"

With a sigh, I followed her until she stopped at a bedroom and opened the door.

A king-sized bed stood against the window. Basically, the most unsafe and stupid place to put a bed, but I bit my tongue. A flat screen took up much of the far wall. A white duvet covered the bed, along with a few red pillows, but other than that, the room was completely bare. No dresser, no chair.

"I won't be sleeping." I nodded to the room. "But thank you."

She frowned up at me. "What? Are you some kind of vampire?"

Would you let me bite you if I said yes? "No."

"I was kidding," she said slowly. "As in, joke. I don't believe in vampires, I'm not..." Was she blushing? It was hard to tell in the dark. "I mean, I read *Twilight* once, but it's not like I obsess about them."

"You ramble when you're nervous."

"I'm not nervous."

"You're blushing."

"It's too dark to tell," she said quickly, crossing her arms.

I smirked. "Renee, it's okay to like vampires. It's okay to like coloring too—"

She scowled.

"I kill people—for money. Do you really think I'm in a position to judge anyone?"

She swallowed. I found myself staring. Why was I having such a hard time with her? We were both acting awkward, and I knew it was because of what Nixon said. Hell, I didn't even want to know what she thought of me.

"If you're sleeping..." I tried steering the conversation, mostly because I wanted to keep talking to her, wanted to see if I could make her blush again. "...then I'll be up watching."

Her eyes widened.

"Not you!" I said quickly. Shit. Hell. Damn. Fuck. "I meant—"

"For monsters who are apparently out to break into my house and kill me in my sleep?"

"Yes. That."

"Well, I'd try to get some sort of sleep if I were you, or it's going to be a long day tomorrow. Besides, I'm not important. I promise." Her smile gutted me; her expression so believing of the words—that she wasn't important.

"You are," I whispered.

Her eyes struck me then. They saw through me, they locked on and didn't let go. And I stared back, I covered my secrets, I buried my scars, and I let her look and hoped she wouldn't see it all.

If anyone wasn't important, it was me.

But Renee?

I might as well be guarding royalty.

"What aren't you telling me, Vic?" she asked in a shaky voice.

"Nothing." I shrugged. "I just take my job seriously." *I take you seriously.*

My eyes flickered to her lips before I straightened and then held out my fucking hand. "Thanks for the bed—" I groaned. "The room.

Thanks for the room. Have a good night."

She stared down at my hand and then took it in hers. It was all I needed. Just to touch her skin, to feel her.

My brain and body were at war, which just meant my mouth wasn't saying the words I was supposed to and rather than come across as elusive and protective, I was coming across like a well-read stalker who lied to get an invite into her room.

"Okay." She dropped my hand.

I hated it.

I wanted her hand back.

I wanted to press her against the wall.

A vibrating sound jolted me out of my lust-filled misery. She pulled out her phone and smiled.

I wanted her to look at me that way.

Not her iPhone.

"It's my mom!" She answered the phone and started talking so fast my head spun. She left me in that doorway. Staring at a bed I wanted to use. Wishing for a life I couldn't have.

And wondering how much I would have to sacrifice to take what felt like the first real want I'd ever had in my existence.

Her.

Chapter Five

Renee

My mom wasn't coming home.

I tried not to sound disappointed on the phone, but she said she was having such a good time and it was working wonders for her anxiety. She missed Dad like crazy and apparently had heard from him.

Another month.

Another month and he would finally be home.

I chewed on that thought.

What kind of job kept him away for a month? I mean, it wasn't like they had mafia conventions where he taught a panel on tax evasion, right?

I tossed and turned for an hour before falling asleep and for some reason, I felt less safe than had Vic been gone.

Everything about him was intense.

His stupid handshake had been intense.

Who has an intense handshake?

How is that even possible?

I hated that what made me close my eyes was the faint smell of him still in the air.

* * * *

"Stay very still," a voice whispered in my ear.

I jolted awake with a gasp, only to have Vic cover my mouth with his massive hand. He was on the floor next to me like he'd crawled in there to make sure no monsters were waiting under my bed.

My heartbeat pounded in my ears as footsteps creaked down the hall.

Someone was in my house.

Someone was in my house.

Were they looking for my dad?

For me?

Blood pounded in my ears as I waited. My chest was so tight that it was getting harder and harder to breathe as the quiet footsteps neared.

"Shhhh." Vic's voice. I closed my eyes and focused on Vic's voice, only to open them just as a man in all black walked by my doorway.

The gunshot rang out before I could suck in another breath, hitting the pillow I'd just been hugging, missing me by inches.

And then another gunshot that came from Vic, from his gun, his hands. The man fell to the ground.

Another stepped into my room. Vic stood and shot him between the eyebrows. Blood exploded against the pretty white walls. I held in my scream. I held it in because there could be more.

My mouth was open.

No sound was coming out.

No air going in.

Vic quickly sat on the bed and pulled me onto his lap. "Breathe, you need to breathe, Renee."

I shook my head as a few tears squeezed out. I was trying! I couldn't get my body to do anything—I was frozen.

Frozen in terror.

Vic swore.

And then he kissed me.

No, no it wasn't a kiss.

It was a claiming.

"Come on," he said between kisses. "Breathe me in, just me, focus on me." His next kiss was light as he blew across my lips. I reacted. I sucked in a breath and leaned forward and then started sucking on him, on his taste, desperate for the safety of his body, desperate for the promise of more kissing—more air.

I molded my body to his, I let him protectively hold me in his lap, and I let myself get lost in something so good.

After seeing so much bad.

I'd been protected from this life.

I knew why now.

It wasn't like a video game. Or a movie.

It was real.

I would never forget the sight of someone getting shot, and it would haunt me for the rest of my life.

Vic's tongue slid past my lower lip.

He tasted hot.

Like any minute his mouth was going to set fire to my body in the best way, burning in my veins, pounding through my blood. I kissed him harder, I clung to him with white knuckles.

And then he was pulling back and wiping tears I didn't realize I'd shed. His thumbs brushed across my cheeks. His clear blue eyes darted between my mouth and my damp cheeks then finally settled on something behind me, like he was afraid to look directly at me.

"You're safe," he whispered in a hollow, unaffected voice. Hadn't we just been kissing? Intimately? "I'll always protect you." He stood.

I grabbed his hand. "Why did you kiss me?"

He looked away, his profile dangerously sharp, his lips full from our shared kiss. Men like him shouldn't look appetizing.

He was chocolate soufflé.

And I felt like boring white ice cream melting all over the place, thanks to my panic.

"Kissing or death." He smiled down at the floor and then looked over at me and winked. I felt my entire body melt. The killer winked and my body buzzed because of it. Shock. I was clearly going through shock. "I figured given the choice you would have said kiss—then again, what do I know?"

"Thank you." I tried not to sound disappointed. Something was very wrong with the way my body swayed toward his, the way that my heart throbbed painfully in my chest like it was going to explode. This was the man who terrified me.

This was also a man who, for the first time in my short life, made me feel alive.

"Renee?"

"Yeah?" I jerked my head up, teeth chattering a bit as the circumstances of my house and bedroom started to choke me.

He pulled out his phone and hit a button. "I think your taste is the only thing that could both save a sinner—and cause more sin."

I gaped just as a male voice answered on the other end.

"Yeah." Vic was all business. "Two intruders…."

My stomach rolled as my eyes found the gory scene and locked on it, unable to look away from the blood splatters and the two bodies that no longer had souls just lying there a few feet away from my bed.

Tears filled my eyes again.

"…I'm not so sure that's a good—" Vic swore again. "Fine, just…Nixon…" His jaw clenched as he glanced back at me like he was in pain. "All right. Fine. Yes. Sorry." And then Vic groaned. "I'm hanging up now. Tell Sergio, and I'm murdering you in your sleep."

I heard laughter on the other end.

Vic shoved the phone back in his pocket. "We need to pack your stuff."

"Pack?" I repeated dumbly. "Why are we packing?"

"Because…" He walked over to my closet and pulled the doors open. "You're coming with me."

"But this is my home! I'm staying here." I jumped off of the bed, ready to fight for the right to stay where I belonged even though I knew I wouldn't sleep a wink. I was getting taken from my home, from what should be my safe space. If I didn't have my home what did I have?

He stiffened. "Not anymore, you're not."

"Vic, be reasonable!"

He turned around and gripped me by the shoulders. "You could have died. How's that for reasonable? Had I not bulldozed my way into your home, the world would have had one less light—one less soul. And don't for one second think they would have made it quick. They would have taken their time with your body, used every last innocent piece you possessed, then made you watch while they slowly snuffed you out of this world. That's reasonable. That's reality. So pack your shit."

My body jolted at his harsh tone. "Where are we going?"

"Nixon's," he whispered. "It's the safest place for you right now."

"Why do I need protection," I wondered out loud, "if they were after my dad?"

He snorted out a humorous laugh. "They weren't after him, you can't be that stupid."

I raised my hand to slap him, but he grabbed it before I could land one against his cheek and shoved me away. "Hit me and you won't like the consequences."

More tears filled my eyes. "I hate you."

He barked out an angry laugh. "Thanks for the reminder."

I instantly felt guilty.

Only because his face had contorted with pain.

Only because his kiss had been the best kiss of my life.

Only because I knew he was doing his job and I was punishing him for it.

"I'm sorry. I shouldn't have—"

"It's fine," he interrupted. "I'm used to people's hate, not really sure what I would do if I had anything else. Pack your things, and be ready in five. And, Renee?"

I was still processing what he said. "Yeah?"

His eyes softened. "You're not coming back."

Chapter Six

Vic

"Is this a new thing?" Chase smirked. "Kissing your captives and all?"

I'd been back at Nixon's for the total of ten minutes before Chase gave me a suspicious look and then another for good measure.

Something was extremely wrong with Chase doing a doubletake where I was concerned. Hell, for the better part of a few weeks he hadn't even known I was in the same house as him, and now he was looking through me like he knew what I'd just done—what I was still thinking about doing the minute we were alone again.

I ignored his comment.

Which wasn't new.

His smile widened as he poured himself a glass of wine then leaned back and stared me down.

The crazy in his eyes never really left.

And the determination in my stare only encouraged it.

The front door opened.

Tex walked in with Phoenix, Sergio, and Dante. I never had to turn around when Tex entered the building. For one, he walked loud, for two, he spoke even louder, as if the entire world needed to pay attention.

I stared straight ahead, straight at Chase, shooting him a challenging glare, and waited for him to start firing off questions about the men I'd killed.

Instead, the minute—no, the second—Tex pulled up a chair, Chase said, "He kissed her."

All heads turned in my direction.

I narrowed my eyes. "Where's your proof?"

"I know what guilt looks like." He leaned forward, resting his tattooed forearms on the table. "And you have it all over your face. Hell, I can even smell it on you—and for the record...next time you decide to kiss the nanny—make sure you wipe the dazed expression off her face and give her some Chapstick for the swollen lips." He winked.

Tex burst out laughing. "At least tell me you killed the men first, kissed her second?"

"Bad ass if he kissed her during," Dante quipped. "Just saying."

Phoenix stared me down. "You know why she's under our protection."

"Yeah," I said gruffly. "I know why. Shouldn't she?"

He pressed his lips together in a firm line and shrugged.

It was midnight. I was exhausted. I needed sleep. And my body was still humming from the taste of her.

It was wrong.

I knew I could never have her—shouldn't even touch her.

I cleared my throat and nodded to Chase. "It won't happen again, you have my word."

"I hate it when people lie to my face." Chase's good humor vanished. "What do you say, Sergio? A thousand? Two?"

I glared straight ahead, and my finger twitched for my gun.

Tex was the first to speak up. "Nah, I say three."

"Five." Phoenix nodded to me. "I bet five against him."

"I'll take that bet." Dante laughed while Tex reached for the wine bottle.

"What are we betting on?" came Nixon's voice as he walked into the room, looking as tired as I felt, and sounding a hell of a lot better than my gravelly sleep-lacking voice.

"Vic sleeping with the help." Chase lifted his wine glass in the air. "Cheers."

Nixon turned his icy expression toward me and muttered a simple "No."

"I didn't do anything...wrong." My cousin stared at me like he was contemplating my death. And I hoped to God I was staring right back as if I'd like to see him try.

I might not be a boss.

But my skills far surpassed those of everyone at the table.

That was why I worked for all of the families instead of just one.

I was the enforcer.

I was whoever they needed me to be.

Tonight I was a babysitter.

Tonight I was an assassin.

I liked babysitting a hell of a lot better.

"Vic." Nixon shook his head no and then paused and looked around the table. "How certain are we that the men were De Lange?"

The front door slammed and Russian boss Andrei Petrov waltzed in wearing a suit. The man didn't own jeans.

In fact, he didn't own anything he couldn't fine press with an iron or by sheer willpower of his palms.

I often wondered who at that table hated him the most.

And then I'd wonder if it matched the hate he felt for himself.

"They were mine."

He took a seat at the same time as I reached for my gun. Nixon shook his head at me.

"And they went against my orders," he continued breezily. "I hope you dealt with them like I've dealt with those they hold dear?"

That was when I noticed the blood on his collar and a scratch near his left ear.

"May God have mercy on their souls—" Andrei poured a glass of wine and lifted it into the air. "Because I didn't."

"Is that lipstick or blood?" Tex pointed to Andrei's collar.

Andrei smiled politely. "After tonight, it's truly a toss-up, but your concern is noted."

Tex pulled out his gun and spun it on the table. "How about a bit of Russian Roulette?"

Andrei jerked to his feet. "You dare threaten me?" Ah, the temper of a nineteen-year-old forced to grow up too soon.

"Stop." Chase gave the command with an eerie calm. "Andrei, why were your men after someone under our protection?"

He sat back down and shrugged out of his suit coat. "Because your man has been feeding me information for the past two months, and the road always has a dead end. We figured he probably came crawling back to the Nicolasi family with secrets of his own—and you know how we do business."

Chase gripped the stem of his wine glass and shot Andrei a look of pure hatred. Nobody liked playing nice with the Russian. We did it out of force, out of necessity and even though he was currently on our side—nobody knew how long it would last or how deep Andrei was willing to go before he completely lost whatever soul he had left.

"She's a nanny, a fucking college student, leave her alone, Andrei." I spoke up for the first time that night, again earning everyone's stares. And even as the words left my mouth I knew they weren't altogether true, even though I wished they were.

Normal would never be in her vocabulary. Not anymore.

He sighed in my direction. "Nixon, if you can't keep your dog on its leash, at least give it something to chew on."

"Or kiss," Tex just had to add.

Andrei's eyebrows shot up. "Kiss?"

"Never mind."

I cleared my throat, only to have Chase follow up with, "He kissed her. Can't kill a girl who's under the protection of any of our names, tough shit, Petrov."

"It was a mistake." He shrugged. "Most likely just as the kiss was… You're what, eight years older than her? What use does a beautiful woman have with a made man who answers to everyone—when she could have someone who answers to no one?"

I clasped my hands in my lap and bit my tongue until I tasted blood. If he so much as looked in her direction, I would end his life.

I would end it with a smile on my face, and no prayer for any part of his soul would do any good.

Andrei stood. "It's been…interesting as usual. When are we moving in on the rat and his family?"

"The rat has been dealt with," Phoenix answered smoothly.

"And his family…" Sergio spoke up for the first time that night. "…will not suffer the full consequences of his actions."

"You can't protect her forever," Andrei said matter-of-factly. "And I'm not the only one you need to be worried about."

I stiffened.

I knew that.

We all knew that.

How was it that the minute we thought we had flushed out all of our enemies, another one rose up, more powerful, more hell-bent on destruction?

"Andrei." Nixon barked out his name. "At least try to do what you swore to us you would do—get in, get out, get done."

"Why?" He snickered. "When I'm having so much fun while I'm in?"

"Gross." Tex shook his head. "Even for you."

Andrei just grinned and started to whistle. The sound of the door slamming jolted me out of my anger—sending white-hot rage to settle over my body.

"Vic." Nixon put his hand on my shoulder. "You're not sleeping tonight. Make sure she's safe, guard the room. If you hear anything—"

"I know how to do my job... Besides, should you really question me when your second-in-command didn't even know I was living with him this last year?"

"That was a choice!" Chase called. "And you're a bagel-stealing monster, I need those!"

I grinned. I knew exactly what he needed them for.

That was why I had found some with tiny holes.

"And Vic." Nixon lowered his voice. "This stops now. You can't start anything with her that you can't finish. Your life isn't meant for..." He sounded sad. He knew the choice I'd made. "Your life will never be normal, you know the vow you took. I can't let you out of it knowing that our family won't be protected. You chose this, now I need you to follow through."

"You can count on me," I said. I lied though. Because for the first time since before taking that oath two years ago—an oath of celibacy when I swore that I would be completely fixed on the families—I suddenly realized why Nixon and Tex had made me do it.

They took away my addiction and gave me focus.

Purpose.

Women had always been a welcome distraction—and they needed me anything but distracted.

I'd stopped partying, stopped traveling, stopped wasting my life with woman after woman... I'd sold my yacht.

I'd sold everything.

Including my soul to the families.

And now, now, I hated that a part of me...wanted it back.

Because of a girl who let me hold her when she was scared.

And who let me kiss her tears away.

Chapter Seven

Renee

"So, do you have everything you need?" Trace, Nixon's wife, clapped her hands in front of her and offered me one of her polite yet guarded smiles. I imagined she spent a large amount of time trying to appear calm in the midst of the mafia storms.

I did a small circle and shrugged. "Sure."

It was a lie.

I needed more than a few pieces of clothes and the turtle my dad gave me when I was little.

"You're going to live here now," he whispered in a hoarse voice. He had tears in his eyes as he pulled my mom close. "I'm going to be your new daddy."

I didn't understand the words at the time. I wasn't sure why I held onto that memory so tightly.

"Safe." My mom repeated the word like it was important. So I said it too. They both looked down at me and smiled.

Tears filled my eyes.

I needed my dad.

I needed my mom.

I needed my life back.

I didn't feel safe.

And I needed the images of those men to stop re-appearing whenever I let my guard down.

Instead, I forced a smile I didn't feel like forcing and waited for her to leave. But she didn't leave. It was like she took my smile as an invitation. Great. She sat on the bed and patted it like I was one of her kids.

I sat. Mainly because I was tired of standing and if I kept thinking about all the blood I was about to pass out anyway.

"Is Vic coming back?" I asked just as she parted her lips and then pressed them together like I'd done something wrong.

"Yes." She swallowed and stared down at her hands. "He's coming back to guard your door."

I sighed in relicf.

"Renee, Vic isn't…You're here because…" She shook her head and tried again. "Vic is here to protect the families, to protect you, us, the kids. He's the best we have, and he can't lose focus."

"Then I promise not to seduce him in my sleep," I said sarcastically. "Scout's honor."

Her eyes narrowed. "Really? Because I was under the impression that something happened between you two."

"Why would you be under any sort of impression when you don't know what happened?"

Trace opened her mouth then closed it. "Just…" She patted my leg. "Just… God, if I can't even talk to you about this, how am I going to talk to my little girl?"

"Ah." It dawned on me in a painfully clear and amusing way. "Just don't let him take my pants off? Is that where this is going?"

She grinned. "I was going for more like 'just be careful because he's not who you think he is and could end up hurting you.'" Her smile fell. "And the opposite could happen too, where you hurt him and he can't work for us anymore. He took an oath."

"What sort of oath?"

"The binding sort." She stood and wiped her hands on her jeans and then hung her head. "I'm sorry, Renee, I really am."

"For what? There are lots of things to be sorry for."

She grimaced. "Let's just say I'm sorry for what happened and even more sorry for what's to come."

My heart thundered in my chest. "What are you talking about?"

"Get some rest." She rubbed her hands together then walked over to the light and flipped the switch, blanketing me in darkness.

I didn't move.

I sat on the bed, my feet touching the floor, my hands folded in my lap. My heart beat louder than my thoughts, my thoughts a jumbled mix of terror and fear.

"Hey." The sound of Vic's gravelly voice made me jump. He pushed the door open a bit more, and light from the hallway spilled in. "Why don't you get some sleep?"

"Right." I stared down at my shaking hands even though I could barely see them. No matter how hard I tried, they trembled. "I'll just stop thinking about all the blood and the fact that I'm in a stranger's house. That one parent is God knows where while the other's in Vegas—don't get me wrong. I'm glad they weren't at the house, but still."

He sighed. "Sometimes you just want your parents—the people closest to you."

"Yeah." For having the physique of a competitive body builder he sure moved fast. One minute he was in the doorway, the next he was on his knees in front of me.

He pressed his massive hands over mine. They were warm to the touch, comforting. Slowly he raised his head and locked eyes on me. "Don't force the fear away, Renee."

"I don't understand."

"The best way to get over fear is to embrace it head on. Don't try to push the thoughts away, let your mind replay them, let your soul feel them, deal with it now so you don't deal with it later."

"Is that what you do?"

He looked away. "Some of us have seen too much for it to work anymore."

"What do you do then?"

He grimaced. "I replace it with a new memory—a fresh kill—and it takes care of the last one. Each memory replaces the last until everything's just a blur."

"That wasn't very encouraging," I murmured, staring at his mouth.

His lips twitched. "Yeah, I had good intentions coming in here. I took a wrong turn when I told you it didn't work—I should have lied."

"No." I gripped his hands in mine. "I'd rather have your truth."

He swallowed. I watched the movement with heavy eyes. Even his massive neck was pretty. He bowed his head a bit then inhaled, fast and deep, and stood. "Sleep."

"You'll be watching?" I asked in a hopeful voice.

"I'll be watching."

"But not in a creepy way," I added.

His smile was faint, but it was there. "In the least creepy way I can muster."

"Thanks, Vic."

"You don't have to thank me for doing my job." He tilted his head and then closed the door behind him.

I could see the shadow of his feet in the light from the hall. He was quite literally standing in front of the door like a prison guard.

With a frown, I hurried and got ready for bed in the dark, then crawled under the covers.

It was an immaculate room.

The bed was soft.

The sheets felt silky against my skin.

But I wasn't home.

I squeezed my eyes shut and wondered if I'd ever be able to utter that word and mean it again.

Chapter Eight

Vic

My eyes burned as I stared ahead at the wall. No distractions. No games on my phone. Just silence and the promise of sleep in the morning once there were more men present at the house. I hated that my thoughts were just as dangerous, as if I had a distraction.

I let out a sigh. Only a few more hours.

I yawned behind my hand.

Checked to make sure my gun was loaded, and I was just putting it back into its holster when Renee screamed.

I barged into the room, gun pointed, eyes searching for an intruder I could end when I realized the window was closed and she was still asleep.

Shit. I quickly put the safety back on and walked over to the bed, where the beautiful, untouchable woman tossed and turned, whipping her hair left and right.

It looked silky against the white pillow.

"Renee," I whispered.

She moaned and then reached for my forearms, her nails digging in like I was enemy number one and she was going to end my life by scratching the skin off my body.

"Renee." I tried again, this time louder.

When her eyes opened, she jerked away from my touch faster than a gunshot. I tried not to take it personally—that she viewed me as the same sort of monster, just a different cause, a different family. I was just like those men—except better at my job.

"Sorry." She pressed a hand to her forehead. "Sorry, I just... You were there, and the men made it into the room, but this time they pulled my ankles and I fell onto the ground, and you yelled at me..." Tears streamed down her face. She lifted a shaky hand to her cheeks. "I don't know if I can go back to sleep."

I couldn't tear my eyes away from her. My body told me to run out of that room, to run from temptation. "You need rest."

"I know!" she snapped and then hung her head. "Sorry, that was uncalled for."

"You were shot at. Pretty sure everything's called for," I said softly. I lifted her chin with my fingertips. Her skin felt soft against the pads of my fingers, and she was warm to the touch.

Breath stalled in my lungs as she stared at my mouth like she wanted to know if it was okay to touch me too.

Run. I needed to run.

I'd already blurred the line.

Nothing good would come of this.

And I'd sworn to the families.

Sworn an oath in blood.

My loyalty had never been tested in such a violent or ridiculous way. A kiss. One kiss had me questioning whether or not I wanted to break a bond worth killing me over.

I had no doubt in my mind, if I crossed this line with her, if I continued to cross it, if I became emotionally involved...

I would be punished.

And I still didn't move my hand.

I still licked my lips and watched her mirror the action.

"Sleep," I finally croaked out. "If it helps, I'll pull up a chair and sit in the room with you." I'd burn in hell for it and probably get shit from the guys, but for her? Anything.

"Yes." She exhaled like she was relieved. "You know I used to be scared of you?"

I smirked. "Noooo, had no clue."

"Are you..." She frowned, then scrunched up her nose. "Are you making fun of me?"

I shrugged. "Maybe."

"So you have a sense of humor, you just keep it on lockdown because you'd rather scare small children and pets?"

I barked out a laugh. "First of all, the kids love me."

She grabbed a pillow and hugged it. "Fine, I'll give you that."

"Second…" I pulled the chair to the side of her bed and sat. "I don't have time to be a comedian. My job is important, my focus is—" I looked away, damn it. "—it's just important that I have no distractions."

"That sounds fun," she said dryly.

"Life is fun for other people…I let them have the fun…my one sacrifice isn't so large to make for the greater good of the families—so that those kids grow up with parents. My job is to make sure that it's not just a fantasy but their reality."

I wasn't sure but it looked like tears were welling in her eyes again. She quickly looked away and got under the heavy blankets and yawned.

"Hey, Vic?"

"Yeah." I crossed my arms and tried to relax but it was getting increasingly harder to do so when she was in bed, talking to me, showing me images of what it would be like—if I was by her side.

She'd be soft.

Warm.

She was a squirmer.

I liked it.

She hugged her pillows and spread her body out like she owned the entire mattress—she'd probably steal my covers. I'd wake up freezing my balls off—and I'd smile because I'd love every fucking minute of it.

"What oath did you take?"

I froze.

She peered over at me, her face innocent, her question like a knife to the gut. Telling her would be the final nail in my coffin, wouldn't it?

Hell, I was already buried, might as well toss the dirt on and get it over with.

With a sigh, I sat forward, pressing my forearms into my thighs. It was almost impossible to see the ink that decorated my arms though it was another reminder of the oath I had taken. I leaned in and showed her my right hand. My patron saint was inked out with blood and around his body the names of each family I'd sworn an oath to protect. "My saint is Joseph…" I licked my lips. "He protects against holy death, destruction, he enforces." I pointed to the family names. "If a war breaks out, if we are attacked and God forbid someone cleanses a line, I would need to cut their name from the back of my hand. I swore fealty to the families, the way a priest swears his life to the church."

Her eyebrows drew together in a frown. "Wait...you mean hypothetically, right?"

"Hypothetically." I pulled my hand back so I wouldn't have to say it that close to her, so I wouldn't smell the perfume on her skin, or the way it mixed with the detergent used for the sheets. "No. I mean that literally. The mafia owns me. Body and soul."

"Is that legal?" she whispered.

I cracked a smile. "I don't really think us murderers care about legal."

"You're not a murderer."

"Your lie isn't necessary. I know what I am." I couldn't look her in the eyes anymore. "I took an oath that will keep my focus on the most important thing." I shrugged. "Keeping you safe. Keeping them alive. Keeping this dynasty running."

She was quiet. I thought maybe she'd gone to sleep, but she let out a loud sigh and then asked, "So you don't have relationships."

"No."

"And you're not allowed to." Her eyes lowered briefly before she jerked her gaze away and hugged her pillow again.

I barely suppressed a smile. "No."

"So you do what in your free time then?"

"That's an easy answer..." I leaned forward again, this time allowing myself the pain of near blinding arousal as I inhaled her scent. "I watch the nanny."

Chapter Nine

Renee

"Junior!" I scolded him as he crawled over to Serena and tried hitting her on the leg. Her lower lip quivered. I waited for the wail.

She sucked in her tears, stared him down, and lifted her chin in the air.

My eyebrows shot up. Good luck with that one, Nixon, if she looked that regal even as an eighteen-month-old? Well, I couldn't imagine what she would be like when she was a teenager.

I scooted a few blocks toward Junior and handed Serena her doll and then felt my entire body start to buzz with awareness.

I pushed the feeling aside.

I'd been edgy all day.

Ever since last night.

And my nightmares.

And waking up to see Vic gone.

I had completely panicked, shot straight out of bed, and run to the door, only to see someone else standing there.

Of course I'd demanded to know where Vic was.

The stranger had said he was taken off duty at six a.m. to get some sleep.

It was one in the afternoon, and I still hadn't seen or heard him.

I rubbed my arms and smiled as Junior struggled to put more than three blocks on top of one another. He was easily frustrated but never gave up. He attacked things in a way that was scary smart, and if he didn't figure it out, he'd stay there all day.

I knew his behavior sometimes concerned Phoenix.

What man wanted to pass on his own demons to his son?

I hugged my knees and then I felt it—like someone was staring at me. With a gulp I turned to the right. Nothing. The left. Nothing. It was just us in the living room.

"He's getting big," came Vic's smooth voice.

I jumped a foot and glared as he approached from the kitchen. "You scared me!"

"Thought you knew I was here," he rasped, his eyes locking on the goose bumps on my arms.

"It's cold." I lied. I wasn't cold. Was my body just responding to him without warning now?

He must have doubted me—I was starting to notice his little quirks, the way his eyes spoke what his mouth refused to confess. His lips twitched when he was amused, and he pressed his lips down to keep from laughing, as if laughing was an unwanted distraction, just like other distractions not allowed by his oath.

I wondered about his life in college and what could possibly take a man from someone who apparently slept with college professors and the rest of the campus, to someone who seemed almost afraid to smile and enjoy life. I wanted to reach up and run my hands over his short jet-black hair. I wanted to ask him if he'd ever grown it past his ears like Sergio. I wanted to find out if he found joy in anything other than taking lives and being scary good at it.

He knelt down and helped Junior with the blocks. Junior sighed and then patted him on the leg as if to say thank you.

Vic's black pants and black tank looked so out of place. As did the weapons strapped to both his chest and his shoulder blades, like he was ready to go to war at any second.

"Got any grenades in there?" I joked.

Slowly he angled his head, giving me another look at that sharp jaw, the one that would slice my fingers open if I wasn't too careful. "Yes."

Oh my. I felt the blood drain from my face.

And then he leaned closer and winked. "Kidding. But I do love a good grenade—it's just...messy."

"That's the only reason you don't carry them around?" I asked in a strangled voice.

He shrugged and then nodded toward the kids. "That and I don't want sticky hands pulling pins."

"Smart," I breathed out.

He inclined his head and stood to his full height, crossing his arms. "Almost nap time."

"You know their schedules?" I grinned.

"No." He sobered. "I know yours."

My body gave an involuntary shiver.

"You're still exhausted," he said softly. "I'll help put them down and then I'll tuck you in…"

My face erupted into giant flames that probably said *hey, you coming too, big fella?* "Um, that's not necessary."

"When it comes to you, everything is necessary."

"You've never been this protective before?" I said it like a question, and immediately regretted it. Did I want to know the truth? His truth?

"Nixon gave me a new assignment this morning." He picked Junior off the floor and growled into his neck then placed a kiss on his nose. His smile was so wide, I almost collapsed into a puddle of worthless heat. It humanized him—holding a child, teasing the child, kissing.

I gaped for a minute before recovering. "So you're leaving soon?"

"Nope." He turned his smile toward me. It slowly dissipated into the most intense look a man had ever given me. "He assigned me to you."

My knees knocked together a bit. "Oh."

"Let's get these guys ready, and then, Renee?"

"Hmm?"

"You will take a nap."

"Is that an order?"

"Yes."

I narrowed my eyes. "And if I say no?"

"Don't make me force you—it won't be pleasant for either of us," he said in a harsh voice. "Besides, I was awake while you slept, I heard your moans, your screams. I watched you suffer when your mind should be resting. Right now, my main concern is you recovering from something you should have never had to see, let alone experience. All right?"

I nodded. "'Kay."

"Good."

I grabbed Serena off the floor and called after him. "You always get your way?"

"Yup!" He didn't even turn around. Junior waved at me like we were playing a game, and I wondered if it was true.

Was this real? A game? Where was my dad? Why was someone trying to kill me? What was so important that they felt the need to assign me one of their best bodyguards? An assassin trained for death dealing.

Why me?

The thought lingered the entire way to the kids' rooms.

And later, when Vic truly did tuck me into bed and turn off my light only to stand outside my door, I chewed on the thought.

The only reason he was here.

The only reason I was there.

Wasn't a small reason.

And I had a right to know.

Chapter Ten

Vic

There are things you know you won't survive. Take a gunfight for example. You go into it knowing that you might not make it out. It causes you to have sharper senses, to make sure that you play a good offense—just as good as your defense.

When I walk into family dinners, I know that it's going to get ugly; too much wine is flowing, and everyone is armed. Plus, Italians. Enough said.

When I walked out of Nixon's office this morning…

I had that same feeling. I responded in the same way. My laser-like focus was intense as hell when I walked into that living room.

And within two seconds.

She unmanned me.

Disarmed me.

By simply existing.

I no longer had weapons.

I had no defense, and my only offense was to put a damn child in front of my body so I didn't do something stupid and use her as my shield—the very thing that had unarmed me.

I pressed my fingers into my temples and leaned against the wall. She needed sleep. Focus on one thing at a time.

Focus.

I opened the door a crack and listened.

Deep breathing.

I sighed in relief then shut the door and braced myself against it.

So easy. To let myself in.

To lock everyone out.

To tell her I needed to taste her again.

To let her mouth haunt me forever.

"Fuck." I banged my head lightly against the wall a few times and then ran my hands over my buzzed hair.

"Trouble in paradise?" Chase leaned against the opposite wall, his eyes narrowed in on the door behind me. "You know sexual frustration can be debilitating…some might argue it's better to just get it over with so you can get your focus back. Because right now? You look slightly insane. And take it from a man who's never going to get his full sanity back—waiting is only going to make it worse."

I snorted. "This from the guy I swore to protect?"

He shrugged. "I can take care of myself. We all can. The reason Nixon hired you has nothing to do with us—and everything to do with the fear that someone's going to use his child against him. You're scary as fuck, and he knows that when you focus on a goal, you don't just achieve it—you bulldoze it over and ask for more." He patted me on the back in passing. "Oh, and Vic? What he doesn't know won't kill him—what's one more secret?"

I squeezed my eyes shut. "You're not helping."

"Huh and here I thought I was making things easier, not…" He grinned. "Harder…"

I flipped him off.

He let out a low chuckle. "Just be prepared for the ramifications. None of us sin and get away with it—at least not without punishment—we've all got the scars to prove it."

"Some more than others," I mumbled.

He sobered and looked away. "You know the family has a therapist."

"Bullshit, like you would ever use a therapist!" I roared, but then I remembered that I needed to keep my voice down.

Chase locked eyes with me. "Sometimes a man wants to battle his demons alone. And other times…" His expression became empty. "Other times, a man just wants to let the demon win."

"Yeah."

He didn't say anything else as he walked away.

I'd never gotten close to Chase.

Didn't want his darkness to recognize mine maybe.

Didn't want to admit how much we had in common.

Loss did that to a person.

It turned my sadness into anger.

And the pathetic part? My anger was a hell of a lot more calming than my peace. And Renee wondered why I didn't smile.

It fucking hurt.

That's why.

Chapter Eleven

Renee

I stretched my arms over my head and smiled up at the ceiling. I didn't have any nightmares, but I did dream of sharp jawlines and lips twitching in my direction. I dreamed of black hair, haunting eyes.

I dreamed of a darkness so consuming I just let it swallow me whole. I dunked my head into the black sea and inhaled.

And liked it.

The girl graduating from college this year.

The one who should be thinking about career opportunities, a family.

Not inviting darkness into my heart and locking it there.

Though if any sin was worth committing—it would be him.

I frowned at the window. The blinds were pulled so I wasn't sure how late in the afternoon it was. At least the kids weren't up yet. I reached for my phone to check the monitor.

My hand met an empty nightstand.

In a panic I looked under my pillow, the covers, and then stumbled over the duvet in an effort to run out of the room.

If anything had happened to those kids, I was going to first murder whoever did something and then be murdered.

Tears filled my eyes as I ran down the hall and stopped at the nursery.

Only to find Vic sitting in the rocking chair with Serena.

Junior was gone.

And the murderer was singing a nursery rhyme. "Ladybird, Ladybird, fly away home, your house is on fire and your children are gone. Ladybird, Ladybird…" He stopped and ran a large finger down her nose, then smiled. He smiled.

I sucked in a breath.

He never smiled at people like that.

I was almost jealous of the little girl who had no idea what sort of gift he'd just given her.

"You were tired," he said without looking up. "I can feel your fear and anger from all the way over here."

"I'm not—"

"It's okay. You wouldn't be a good nanny if you weren't panicked. I didn't mean to scare you." He looked up. "I never mean to scare you."

His eyes pleaded with mine in a way that made my heart twist in my chest, like he needed me to understand that it was never his intention to be like one of the monsters in my head—even though he was like them, even though he killed like them.

I nodded. "I know."

He stood. "Junior went home with Phoenix after his nap… Serena was hungry, and Trace wasn't home yet, so I changed her, we ate, read some books, and then watched some Sesame Street. She got bored and decided it would be more fun to tie shoelaces together. We had dinner, made some Play-Doh, and by then it was time to go back to bed. Nixon and Trace wanted to put her down but…" His voice trailed off.

"But what?"

He shrugged. "I was angry—she makes me free."

It was all he needed to say.

It made me both jealous and sad.

I hated both emotions.

"You're really good with her," I whispered.

His eyes flashed with pain so brief that I swore I was seeing things, and then he set her down in her crib and kissed her on the forehead. She had a small stuffed white horse in her crib at all times. Nixon kept it there as a reminder of what they would lose—if betrayed again. I had no idea why. Or what it meant. I just knew that whenever anyone saw her with it, they looked like they were about to either cry or storm off. I was almost afraid to ask. But the mafia dealt with symbolism all the time. It's what they did. I didn't question what I would never understand or be a part of.

A small voice inside me told me that I already was.

That they were hiding something from me.

But I shoved it away.

Summer was almost over.

I had one week left and I'd be leaving for school.

Just like I planned.

And this would just be a brief nightmare followed by the dream of Vic's kiss that I'd carry with me forever.

"You should eat." Vic's voice snapped me out of my thoughts.

I put my hand on my stomach. "You're right. What time is it?"

"Seven."

My eyes widened. "I slept six hours!"

"Shhhh."

I glared like I needed to know when to be quiet. A bomb could go off and Serena would yawn.

I flipped off the light, and darkness settled over us except for the small princess nightlight on the opposite end of the room.

I could hear my heartbeat.

Feel my heavy breathing.

There was something familiar about the darkness. Something exciting about the way it whispered promises of secrecy when I knew that they were a lie.

I hung my head a bit and reached for the door.

Only to have Vic reach around me and press his palm against it, closing us to the hallway.

To the light from the hall.

I closed my eyes as the air moved behind me, as he towered over me. I could feel him behind me. All six foot four of him.

Rough hands weighed down on my shoulders.

And then he was resting his head against mine.

A war began in that room.

Between two hearts.

Between a broken soul.

And a lost one.

I wet my lips.

His hands ran down my arms until they came into contact with my hands. He interlocked our fingers and squeezed tight.

I leaned back against his chest and wrapped his muscular arms around me. I could hear his sigh, I could feel the intensity of the moment. It was in the air between us, it both choked and freed.

It was quicksand.

It was fire.

I eyed the doorknob.

And then he was turning me around in his arms. His blue eyes didn't leave mine. I was afraid to blink. Afraid to snap him out of the tug of war between us.

The kiss. The attraction. The knowledge that he had always been watching.

"I watch the nanny."

My knees knocked together.

"I watch the nanny."

He'd been watching.

Everything.

And as afraid as I'd been—I'd liked it.

Maybe even craved it.

"You're watching again," I whispered.

"You want me to," he responded.

Our mouths met in a crescendo of fire. I parted my lips as the scorching heat of his tongue dragged past my lips. I arched my back as he pressed hungry kisses down my neck. Every touch stirred something terrifying inside me, something my heart clamored for. More. More. More. He kissed with precision, attacked angles I didn't know existed.

He didn't kiss like a college boy.

He kissed like a man.

Every provoking stroke of his tongue had my body blazing out of control. *Walk through the flames,* his kiss said. *Drown while I hold your hand.*

My mouth quivered as I snaked my arms around his neck. He pressed me against the wall, lifting me effortlessly into his arms and setting me on his thigh as his hands reached under my flimsy T-shirt.

"I should stop," he rasped against my parted lips.

"Do you always make the right choice?" I challenged.

He ran a thumb over my nipple. I jerked in response—my bra was thin, I felt like every single part of my body strained toward him, begging for more of what he had.

"What do you think?" He spoke the words against my neck, pulled back, and smiled.

He might as well have wielded that sexy smile as a weapon.

Danger! My heart screamed.

Danger! My mind agreed.

Danger! My body cheered and went back for seconds as I slid my tongue past his lower lip and tasted him, drank the deep damning poison that something between us produced.

I'd never lost myself in a person.

But men like Vic? They made a person want to shut out everything but the tiny moments of you together.

He moved his hand down my stomach to the leggings I was wearing and cupped between my thighs while I kissed him, while I urged him on, riding his hand like we weren't in a mob boss's daughter's room, seconds away from being exposed to the world.

I drove my hips against him.

Curses fell from his mouth.

The bold caress of his tongue was enough to drive me insane.

A soft knock sounded on the door.

We pulled apart so fast I almost fell on the carpet.

"It's just me," Chase whispered. "Didn't see either of you come out. Nixon ran into town, he'll be back in four minutes. Figured that was valuable information..." The humor in his voice was my only solace at the moment. I didn't want to get fired. I also didn't want to get killed for tempting the murderer.

I squeezed my eyes shut. "Yeah, thanks Chase."

"Careful, kids..." His warning was quiet.

I felt slightly insulted that he called me a kid. I was twenty-one.

Vic was at least thirty.

"Sorry." Vic touched my shoulder lightly, and then pulled open the door. "I'm sorry."

"Why are you sorry?"

"Some things aren't worth dying for," he confessed.

"I'm not worth dying for?" Hurt hit me on all sides.

"You misunderstand..." He hung his head. "You're worth all of it—but it's not fair to bring you down to hell with me, just because I can't control myself. It won't happen again."

He walked out of the room.

And a small part of me felt pride that he was walking funny.

And that every muscle in his body was taut like it had been pumped up but not had any sort of release.

I knew the feeling well.

That was stupid.

It was a bad idea.

But being with Vic was the most alive I'd felt—ever.

Of course it would be in a killer's arms where I felt the safest and most alive...a death dealer, giving life. Who would have thought?

Chapter Twelve

Vic

I went into the kitchen in search of something to put my mouth on that wasn't going to get me killed—like oatmeal, cereal, all the alcohol.

I poured a glass of wine and sat down just as Renee made her way down the hall. Fresh faced like she'd just taken off what was left of her makeup, with her hair in a ponytail and gorgeous legs in gray sweats.

She gave me a pensive look before going to the fridge and opening it. I choked on my next gulp when she bent over to grab something.

"You can at least try to be less obvious." Chase sat down next to me.

"You could at least try to keep your fucking voice down," I snapped.

Which just made him grin.

Shit, the guy had a death wish.

"You think I like sitting at Nixon's when I could be home with my wife? She made roast. You know how I feel about roast."

I rolled my eyes. "No, actually I don't."

"Oh, well, let me tell you." Bastard stole my glass and lifted it to his lips. "It's succulent..." He grinned wide. "Moist and just..." He released a long sigh that had me ready to smack him. "So primed and ready... You ever have roast like that? Just melts on your tongue..."

"Fair warning, if I shoot you in the kidney—this conversation proves you deserved it." I stood and grabbed another glass then sat back down.

He drummed his fingertips against the table.

Renee made her way over to us and sat. In the time I'd graphically plotted Chase's murder—she'd made a sandwich.

"So Renee…" Chase smiled at her. Where the hell was a tranq gun when a guy needed it? A muzzle. Anything. "Are you excited to finish school?"

Her face lit up.

Shit. I already didn't want to let her go.

Couldn't even think about facing a day where I couldn't at least watch her, keep her safe. What kind of screwed-up brain was I suffering with? It wasn't just borderline stalking.

It was real shit that got you on Dateline, where friends and family members go, "He was just so attentive to her every need," AKA, he was a fucking stalker.

"I can't wait." She beamed. Shit, she was actually beaming. I stared into my wine and listened to her voice. I told myself her face wasn't alive with excitement. I told myself she was just riding the high of my tongue.

I lied.

"You have what? Five days left?"

"Six," she corrected.

"Clearly you're making the most of it," he commented.

I jerked my head in his direction. "Meaning what?"

His face was innocent. But nothing Chase said or did was ever without reason. He simply shrugged. "Hanging out with the kids. Why? What did you think I meant?"

I clenched my teeth while Chase poured another glass of wine and winked at Renee like he had a right to.

The front door opened. Nixon stomped through and shut it behind him with a bang. "Fucking Russians."

"Here, here." Chase lifted his glass to his lips. "Trouble at the club?"

"He's out of control." Nixon's eyes were wild. He raked a hand through his inky black hair. "Petrov makes me wish for all female kids— that's how much I want to strangle him. He defies us on purpose just to see how far he can push us, and he's a nineteen-year-old piece of shit!"

"Careful, Dante's a boss at twenty," Chase warned.

"Dante listens to you." He nodded to Chase. "He thinks of you as an older brother, you know that."

Guilt flashed across Chase's face. "Yeah, I know."

"Do you need me to go rough him up a bit?" I asked casually. I wouldn't mind the release. God knew I needed one.

Nixon let out a rough exhale. "Don't rough him up, we're not supposed to touch him."

I deflated.

"But..." He grinned. "You can have some fun with his men. Besides, the sick bastard actually likes when others get tortured, even if they're loyal to him."

"Consider it done." I stood.

"One more thing." He glanced at Renee.

My heart dropped.

Did he know?

Could he see the telltale puffiness of her lips?

The heavy rise and fall of her chest?

"I told you we needed to talk, the three of us..." He rubbed his eyes with the palm of his hands. "Renee, you...you aren't returning to school."

Angry tears rimmed her eyes. "What?"

"You're not going." He said it softer, his eyes darting to Chase. "That's final."

"That's final?" Renee crossed her arms. "Who died and made you my father? I want to talk to him. If he says no, then I'll stay."

"You can't," Nixon whispered.

"Why the hell not?" she yelled.

"Your father's dead." Nixon reached across the table and covered her hand with his.

"No." She shook her head. "No, no, you don't understand, he's just out...on business for the Nicolasis. He's not...." Tears streamed down her cheeks.

"Sweetheart..." Nixon squeezed his eyes shut. "He was playing both sides, causing us to lose good men who were in the wrong place at the wrong time. He's been taken care of."

"So you killed him!" she roared.

"No." He blinked over at me.

Fuck. "I did," I admitted.

She sucked in a breath of heavy betrayal and looked away, giving me her back just as I deserved.

"Innocent lives were being lost because of him, Renee. Families were getting exposed." Nixon tried to reason with her. He was still hiding the truth but doing it in the only way that still kept her safe. It didn't matter though. He was her father. It would never matter. We can't control who we love. "It had to be done."

"Did it?" Her voice was heavy with tears.

Shit. I braced myself against the chair.

"Vic?" Nixon nodded to the door. "Go, we'll be fine."

I didn't want to go.

My fingers turned white as I gripped the chair.

Nixon frowned as a war raged in my heart.

He was boss to the richest family in the Cosa Nostra.

He was boss.

And yet I hesitated.

Hesitation meant a swift death.

At this moment he was no longer my cousin or my friend.

He was judge, jury, and executioner.

My needs didn't matter.

My desires could go to hell.

My eyes flickered to Renee. I wanted to draw her up into my arms, kiss her tears, tell her I was sorry that she'd known death twice since knowing me.

So damn sorry.

"Vic," Nixon growled. "I won't ask you twice."

I inclined my head and slammed the door hard behind me.

Let him feel anger.

It was nowhere close to the rage pounding in my body.

Chapter Thirteen

Renee

Tears blurred my vision as I sat in Nixon's office and waited for whatever was supposed to come next. Pictures lined his walls. A dark mahogany desk sat toward the back of the room. The place smelled just as expensive as it looked. I was sitting in a red leather wing-backed chair that was probably heavier than a Ford Focus.

I felt surrounded by choking loneliness in that room.

By death and cold.

I could still feel my father's arms around me, see the look on his face when he promised he would take care of my mom and me.

My hands shook in my lap as Nixon sat back in his chair and stared me down like he wasn't quite sure what to say.

I wiped away a stray tear. "Should I be worried?"

"Worried?" His eyebrows drew together. "About what?"

"Getting killed if I break one of the rules?"

He sighed and looked away from my face, his gaze focused on a picture on his wall. "Renee, I will do anything to protect those who live under my household. I would die for you—any of the men wouldn't even blink. Do you really think so little of us that we would kill you for being human?"

"You killed him."

He bit down on his lower lip, a look of frustration crossing his face. "What if I told you that he got ten people killed, including children? What if I told you he messed up and couldn't find a way out of it? What if I told you I don't even know how it went down because Vic doesn't want to burden me with it—but that I know your dad begged for it?"

"Begged for death!" I yelled.

"Begged for a quick death without suffering—I guarantee he would have suffered for days, maybe even weeks, his wife, children..." His voice trailed off. "Things in our life are not black and white. We exist in a very gray area, constantly asking if the sin justifies those who are saved. This isn't violence to be violent—this is survival for a future. You must understand that. And if you don't? Well then I can't have someone that close-minded watching my daughter. Think about it—and if you want to quit your job, I'll find a safe house for you, but until you turn twenty-two, you will need protection."

"Why twenty-two?" I frowned. "That's in three months."

"In three months we'll be closing in on the holidays. I figured you'd want to be with your mom."

Something wasn't adding up. I narrowed my eyes. "My mom, does she know?"

"Yes."

Betrayal twisted like a knife in my gut. "And she couldn't bring herself to tell me...why?"

"I wanted to talk to you first. To make sure you were okay before she dropped the bomb... Seems like I misjudged the situation—since you would have preferred hearing it over the phone while your mom drank her sorrows away in Vegas—I won't make the mistake again." He nodded to the door.

I stood on wobbly legs and walked over to the door, getting a sudden vision of Vic and me pressed against it, our mouths wild, our tongues tangling.

I watch the nanny.

With a sigh, I grabbed the doorknob and jerked the door open.

Chase was standing there with a bottle of wine in his hand and a glass. He offered them to me. Dark circles rimmed his eyes, his voice sounded tired as he spoke slowly. "Don't take out all your anger on him. He was just doing his job."

I looked away. "His job was to kill my family member."

"No." Chase sidestepped me. "His job was to keep us safe. And he did that. It's not just about the blood that's dead in the ground—it's about the blood still living. Go to sleep."

Excused, I carried the bottle back to my room along with the wine glass and set them both on the nightstand.

The chair from the previous night was still next to the bed.

It was empty.

Tears filled my eyes as I grabbed a blanket and dragged it over to the chair then sat and drew my knees up to my chest. I wasn't going back to school. My father was gone. My life was over.

And still, still I could smell Vic.

Still, I felt his arms wrap around me in my imagination.

How could someone be both your strength and your nightmare?

My eyes fluttered closed on a deep sigh.

Chapter Fourteen

Vic

I knocked on the black metal door three times. It opened, revealing a man in a red head-to-toe suit with a black tie. He was wearing a cape that swept the ground in a way that reminded me of a historical novel.

"Password."

"Club Tempt," I said in perfect Russian.

The door opened wider.

The smell of cigars and expensive cologne filled the air, swirled around my head as I made my way down the familiar halls. Every type of woman hung off every type of man. They all had masks covering their faces, drinks in their hands, and if rap music hadn't been playing, I'd have assumed that I'd gone back in time to a masquerade in underground London.

The men wore top hats, dominos, expensive clothes that would be extremely out of place on the streets. I was completely out of place in jeans and a black cotton shirt.

The carpet was a blood red, and dark flickering candles lit the narrow hallways with their small alcoves where you'd see people snickering and stripping each other.

And then the worst part.

The dangling key on every woman's ankle.

And the lock tattoo that accompanied it.

With a sigh, I made my way down another hall and then into the main dance area where music pumped from loud speakers. Red velvet couches were draped in people half-dressed and groping one another, enjoying each other's company, and drunken kissing. A den of iniquity.

Fun.

Petrov was standing watch in the VIP section like a king looking over his land. A cruel smile spread across his face and then he crooked his finger at me.

I took the stairs two at a time and when a bouncer stared me down and refused to pull back the velvet rope, I gripped him by the neck with one hand and barked, "Problem?"

"No," he croaked.

"Good, good." I slowly pulled my hand away and adjusted his tie then slapped him lightly on the right cheek. "We've got business."

Petrov inclined his head at us. "Leave us, D."

I made my way toward where Petrov was standing over the balcony. "He's charming."

"Isn't he, though?" Petrov grinned. "I find him amusing."

"Dumb as a bag of rocks then?"

"The dumb ones are easier to persuade…and they're fearful they'll never make as much money as what I pay them—the dumb ones keep me safe. They keep what's happening here safe."

I gripped the railings. "Nixon's upset."

He snorted. "Nixon's always upset. What else is new? He said I could handle my business the way I want to, just because I'm slowing down the process doesn't mean I don't mean to take down the empire my father built. But there are key players I need on my side, and I can't just force my hand. Nixon knows this."

I nodded. "He knows it. I know it. The problem is that you're getting in too deep. How many times have you been out on the floor? How many times have you gone to the sales? My information says your hand has been in every part of this little front for slavery—you're in too deep."

He rolled his eyes. "I'm fine."

"Have you slept with any of them?" I asked boldly.

His jaw flexed. "It's not like that."

"Oh, so it's love?"

He slammed his hands down on the railing and then closed his eyes like he was trying to calm himself. "Don't question me."

I turned. "Don't give us a reason to," I whispered in his ear. Then I grabbed his hand like I was going to shake it, and broke his index finger.

It snapped easily.

He didn't cry out.

He just narrowed his eyes at me like he was annoyed I'd just hurt him and he couldn't do anything about it without drawing attention.

"A reminder." I inclined my head. "Of who you belong to. Of what the families will do to you if you double-cross them."

He inhaled a deep breath and held his hand. "Chaos is my control. Let me do things the way I see fit. I've already freed fifty girls. That's fifty fewer girls worrying about drug addiction or getting beat to death."

I nodded. "And the other two hundred?"

"You'll see..." He grabbed a drink from the table with his left hand. "I'll show you all...you think you know everything, arrogant bastard Italians. I have my hand in families across the world. Don't make petty threats you aren't willing to back. Besides, you need this more than I do. I hold the keys to the house. You're simply a buyer in a long line of other buyers who don't walk into my domain and break appendages." He grinned and lifted the glass to his lips. "Have a good night, Vic."

I stared him down, noticing his bluff, wondering why it was necessary. And then I saw a man and woman sitting at the lower bar. A familiar man and woman next to a billion nameless faces, within a minute I was by them, monitoring them, Andrei watching, always watching. We didn't let just anyone into this bar.

"Einstein." I grinned at the beautiful, clever girl who frankly knew too much about our dealings. "Funny seeing you in our city."

Her smile didn't waver. "You didn't seem surprised to see us here."

"I could say the same about you."

"Funny how that works." Her smile was forced as she glanced between me and Andrei then back at me with intensity in her eyes. "Can I assume you know why we're here?"

I flinched, my shoulders barely moving. "You could. You would be wrong."

"We need Phoenix."

I sighed. "Must be bad if you need a Nicolasi who holds all the scary information in every crime family in the world."

Her smile fell a bit.

"Shit, I'll let him know to expect a visit."

"Figured showing up here first to warn Phoenix we were coming would put us on his good side." Einstein tossed back the rest of her drink in one gulp as the guy next to her curled his arm around her waist in possession.

I snorted. "Yeah, keep telling yourself that." I kissed both of her cheeks, nodded to the man next to her and escorted myself from the dark club, hating that I took part of the stench with me into my G Wagon. Hating the slavery I couldn't stop—the slavery we had to support by default before we could bring it down. I saw Renee in those women dancing, the fear in their eyes when they were taken to the back room. Nobody returned from that room. I hated that she looked at me the way those women looked at the men they danced with.

I hated that she really believed I was a monster now that she knew I'd killed her father.

My thoughts were so consuming, I didn't even realize I'd driven back to the house until the iron gates opened.

I parked in the garage and walked into the house. It was quiet. Dark.

"How'd it go?" Nixon asked from the shadowy corner of the living room, like he was waiting up for me.

I tossed my keys onto the table. "As good as can be expected." I frowned then. "Saw one of the Borellos."

"Oh? That's pretty far to travel for a meeting. We don't deal with other family drama. We have enough on our hands." His voice sounded strained, yet curious. "What the hell do they want?"

"Info from Phoenix."

He snorted. "God help us all."

I chuckled and then sobered. "How did it go with Renee?"

"Oh, let's see." Nixon stood and walked over to me. "She yelled, cried, then yelled some more, and then didn't believe me when I told her that her father asked for a swift death rather than torture."

My heart cracked in my chest as I listened.

"I told her you're one of the best men I know, and I'm sorry you were put in that position."

"You would have done the same thing."

"Some days...yes. Others...Well, let's just say seeing others suffer makes you feel a lot better."

Chapter Fifteen

Renee

Heat wrapped itself around my body. It soothed my soul. I think I took my first deep breath in those seconds, my first big exhale, followed by another deep breath. I pressed my hand against the heat, and came into contact with a hard chest. I didn't even care that it was the chest of my father's murderer.

I was sick.

Sick that my murderer made me well.

I wrapped my arms around his neck and breathed him in. We were walking. I didn't want to spoil the moment by speaking, so I kept my eyes closed, my voice silent as he walked and walked some more.

A door opened and closed.

It smelled like cigars and Christmas spices.

Gently, I was being set down. My body came into contact with something deliciously soft, and it wrapped around me.

And then whatever I was on moved, dipped under the weight of the one carrying me. Maybe if I just kept my eyes closed I could imagine that it was Vic without the word murderer hanging over his head like a blazing red sign.

Maybe I could give in to the fantasy that he was just a guy, I was just a girl. Spending the night in each other's arms, using each other's heat for energy.

Blankets were piled over my body, pushing me into the mattress with their weight. And then bulky arms pulled me back against the rock-hard chest again.

"Sleep." His voice carried like a gunshot in the dark; it was a harsh whisper, a command I wasn't allowed to say no to. Sometimes, you just need to be forced into rest—and when he'd walked in, I'd been tossing and turning in that stupid chair trying to get comfortable for hours.

But now? Now my body was heavy. My mind was silent.

"Did you kill anyone tonight?" I asked the dreaded question. I wanted to know if the hands that were holding me were hands that had washed off blood. I'd tortured myself with ideas of what he was really going to do tonight. Tortured myself with visions of my dad's face begging for death.

His body was rigid as he bit out, "No, Renee. I didn't kill anyone tonight."

"Are you going to kill anyone tomorrow?"

He sighed. "Well, it is a Friday, those are my favorite days to take a life. What do you think?"

I smiled even though it wasn't funny. "Sorry, stupid question."

"Which earned an equally stupid answer."

"Hey, Vic?" I turned to face him. His eyes were so bright in the darkness that it startled me a bit before I could gather my thoughts. "Did he really beg you?"

"Don't make me talk about it. Not now. Not when you're tired and upset. Not when you look at me like you're disappointed. I can handle a lot of things, Renee, your disappointment in me is not one of them."

I nodded. "I don't want to be."

"Sometimes we don't have a choice, we just are. You loved your father. I took that away. The details don't matter when you love, only the end result. In this case—the death—it's all that counts, Renee, especially in this life."

Tears filled my eyes as I wrapped my arms around his neck and pulled him close. I kissed the top of his forehead and then the end of his nose. He clenched his jaw like he was trying to calm himself down and doing a crappy job of it.

"Sleep." I smiled sadly.

He blinked and then looked away. I pulled his chin back so he had no choice but to look into my eyes. "Sleep," I urged again. "Or I won't."

"And if someone sneaks into the house and tries to hurt you?"

"At least I'll die by your side, right?"

"No." He pulled away and gripped both of my wrists. "I wouldn't let that happen. Never. I will never let someone take your soul before it's had a chance to love—to live. Never. Do you hear me? Never!"

"You can't control everything, Vic. You should know that by now."

"Which is why I try like hell to at least control what I can," Vic whispered. "Which is you getting the sleep you need so that you're rested and so that I don't decide that it's a good idea to force exhaustion on you."

I frowned. "Force exhaustion?"

He gripped my ass with his right hand, squeezed, and jerked me against his body. "Exhaustion."

"I wouldn't mi—"

He pulled his hand free and cupped it over my mouth. "Not another word. Sleep."

I nodded as his hand slid away, his eyes focused on my mouth like he was telling himself just one taste would be okay.

I was making it harder on him.

To keep his oath.

And he was making it harder on me.

To view him as a monster.

Especially when he looked at me as if I was his savior.

Chapter Sixteen

Vic

I let her sleep in my bed.

And when she didn't wake up after my alarm went off, I let her sleep some more. It seemed like it was the least I could do after killing her father.

"So…" Nixon's voice surprised me enough for me to nearly drop my coffee cup. Normally I was aware of everything around me.

Normally I didn't have a sexy woman sleeping in my bedroom.

They were right about her being a distraction, that was for sure.

"Yeah?" I turned around with a bored expression like I'd known he was there the whole time.

He crossed his inked-up arms against his plain white shirt. "Now that she knows her father is dead, now that she knows the truth—maybe it's best to just rip the Band-Aid completely off?"

"By Band-Aid you mean by telling her why she needs protection twenty-four seven?" I squinted at him.

He rubbed his chin. "Maybe. I'll talk with Tex." He turned on his heel. "Oh, sorry, almost forgot…Trace wants to take Serena downtown. We'll stay at one of the apartments overnight, go shopping. It's… Let's just say a lot of this is a reminder for her. It's a trigger for a lot of us…inviting someone into our home that we have to protect never goes well. They either end up married or dead."

He was right. Whenever we protected someone it was either marry them so they were untouchable, or they ended up being rats or worse…they were taken out by their own body's inability to stay alive.

"Go." I shrugged. "We'll be fine, just take all the extra men with you."

"I know you'll be fine, and we have an army of men coming." Nixon's smile didn't reach his eyes. He turned around, nearly making it out of the kitchen before he called back over his shoulder. "I was watching you for three minutes before you knew I was in the kitchen with you—should I be worried?"

Shame was a bucket of ice water dumped over my entire body, making me go completely rigid as I clenched my teeth and let out a harsh, "No."

"Good. I would hate to find out that one of my favorite cousins can't keep an oath…"

I rolled my eyes. "You said Sergio was your favorite last week."

Nixon just laughed and walked off.

With shaking hands, I set my coffee cup down and slapped my face a bit. I needed to snap the hell out of it before I got myself or someone else killed.

Maybe Chase was right.

Maybe it was because the temptation was there. Maybe I did need to get it out of my system, but the last thing I wanted to do was sleep with her once just to satisfy this craving between us and then go back to normal.

It would be impossible to go back to normal without always wanting her in my arms.

I could always visit the club.

The idea had merit.

It would make Petrov trust us more, plus I would owe him a favor. Bastard always loved holding favors over people—he might as well get my blood on a contract.

It was decided then.

So why was my heart still hammering in my chest? Why was I still dreaming of her mouth, the way her body molded perfectly against mine? Why did my stomach clench thinking about touching someone who wasn't her?

At least she could sleep in and not worry about the kids. I made a quick call to see if Junior was coming over, but Phoenix and Bee were going to bring Junior into town too.

They lived the closest.

I gulped.

That left Chase around two miles away.

Tex ten miles.

Dante and Sergio even farther.

I wiped my hands over my face.

It was fine.

It wasn't like I needed a babysitter to keep it in my pants, right?

Within an hour they were gone.

And I was alone with Sleeping Beauty.

My lips twitched as I walked by my room and heard a soft snore. How the hell even her snore was cute I had no idea. It was close to ten, and I didn't want her waking up thinking that she hadn't done her job.

I walked in the room, careful to keep quiet, and sat down on the bed, then rubbed her arm. "Renee, time to wake up."

She grabbed my hand and held it.

And I just sat there and let her.

She unarmed me in a way that was terrifying.

She unarmed me with hand holding.

I hung my head as she squeezed my fingers tight.

"Renee." I leaned closer. "Time to wake up, sweetheart."

She stirred a bit then opened her eyes, still holding my hand. She didn't let it go as she sat up and pulled her knees to her chest. "What time is it?"

"Ten," I answered just as a panicked expression crossed her face. "Don't worry, everyone's gone."

"Gone." Her eyes widened. "Why are they gone? What happened?"

"Family staycation in downtown Chicago—normally I'd be with them, but they have an army of men, and I needed to stay and take care of you." I knew the silent command from Nixon was to protect her at all costs. Suddenly she was more important than his family, she had to know there was a reason.

She frowned. "I still don't get it. Nixon won't tell me anything, but there's more to this, there's more to my father's deceit. He wouldn't just…hurt the families, you have to believe me."

"On purpose? No. He would not. Then again…maybe he was protecting you by doing what he did. If anything, it brought our attention to him again. It reminded us why he was so important in the first place."

"Because of how good he was at his job?" she asked out loud.

"Because he was in charge of protecting you."

"But he was never home," she said in a confused voice.

Ah, how to explain life and death to someone who only wanted to see life even in the worst situations.

"Renee, your father wasn't just a made man, he wasn't involved in typical business meetings…your father, he had over forty kills to his name—he was sent to Sicily to do…business."

"With who?"

"You should eat breakfast." I stood and let go of her hand. "Do you want toast? Eggs? Ice cream?"

She glared. "I'm not one of the kids."

Her breasts were practically spilling out of her low-cut tank top, and already I could see her toned thighs fucking taunting me with every step she took in my direction. I wanted to lick between them and see how many licks it would take to get to her center. Countless. Licks. "Yeah." I croaked. "I'm aware."

Her eyes flickered to my mouth like she could read my thoughts, and then she breezed past me. "I hope you make a mean egg."

I smiled in that empty room.

The same room I'd felt isolated in for so long.

The same house that had never felt like a home.

And suddenly—because of her, it was all of those things.

Danger!

I squeezed my eyes shut, I clenched my fists, and I stared ahead at the blank white wall.

The one with no pictures.

No memories.

No life.

Dangerous.

She was so fucking dangerous to someone like me, someone who'd lived in darkness so long they had no idea that light was even possible.

Until she flipped the switch.

And smiled.

Chapter Seventeen

Renee

I felt him even when he wasn't in the room. I shivered as I made my way into the abandoned kitchen.

The kids were gone.

It was just me and Vic.

My father's murderer was going to make me eggs.

And I was going to what? Just let him?

I dug my nails into my palms as Vic walked into the kitchen, grabbed a pan, and then went to the fridge.

He moved around me effortlessly like I wasn't even there. I was stuck in a daze of confusion. Not over breakfast.

But over life.

What did that mean for me?

Was my mother aware I was trapped in this house with one of the wealthiest crime families in the world?

Especially after knowing about my father's death?

Did she even know he was a murderer like Vic?

Pieces of a puzzle still fit together once you look at every piece, but I didn't have the pieces. I knew very little. So I had no picture.

And I really, really needed a picture so I could focus on the positive—or find out if that was even possible.

"Eggs are ready," Vic called in his raspy, addictive voice.

I jerked my head up.

He was holding out a plate with a piece of toast and an egg fried in the middle, cut out in a perfect little square.

I smiled. "What's this called?"

"Good food." He shrugged. "The perfect combination of fat, protein, and carbohydrates." He shoved the plate into my hands. "Eat."

"Thank you." I took the blue plate, walked over to the breakfast bar, and sat just in time for him to hold out a fork about two inches from my face. I gripped it in my right hand and dug in.

While he watched me.

As if I could eat an egg the wrong way.

I chewed my first bite and nodded. "You know, if you weren't so good at killing people you could probably be a chef."

"You mean switch from blood to ketchup?"

"Yeah, think of the possibilities."

His smile was sly. I both liked and hated it, mainly because his level of sexiness just kept increasing with each minute I was with him. "What if I like killing people?"

I choked on my next bite.

His massive hand came crashing down on my back like I'd just sucked down a grape.

Slap, slap, slap.

I almost herniated.

"Fine!" I said hoarsely. "I'm totally fine, just...wrong tube."

"You sure?" he asked, hand raised.

I pressed my lips together to keep from laughing. "Yeah, I'm...great."

I hadn't realized how close he was.

Or the fact that his crystal blue eyes had pieces of yellow outlining the irises. In another life he would have been a vampire out to glamour me.

And I would have fallen for it hook, line, and sinker.

"Good." He didn't move.

I cleared my throat and reached for my fork again.

"And no...the answer's no."

I looked up into the depths of his eyes—I looked into his soul. I liked it there, it was the eye of the storm, calm—just waiting to twist into violence. I waited for him to say more.

He let out a sigh. "I don't like being the last thing people see when they leave this earth."

"I guess we'll just have to agree to disagree—because I can't imagine anything better to look at during my last few breaths."

He swayed toward me, then moved behind my stool, bracing his hands on either side of my body, pinning me against the hard granite. "Don't say things like that to me, Renee."

"Why?"

He closed his eyes and inhaled. "Because it's unwise to offer an addict free drugs, that's why."

"So now you're an addict?"

His eyes roamed over my body like a slow burning fire. "All it took was one taste...." He jerked away. "I'm going to check the perimeter. Finish your breakfast."

"Am I allowed to watch TV?"

"Have you finished your chores?" he teased.

My jaw dropped as a laugh erupted from his body in a way that had me wanting to be the cause of it.

"Don't make me throw my fork at you!"

"Cat-like reflexes..."

I threw it.

He literally caught it midair and shrugged then placed it back on the countertop. "And yes, you can do whatever you want...within reason."

"You ever going to tell me why I'm a prisoner here?"

"No."

"So it's not even up for discussion a little bit?"

"No."

"And I can't persuade you?"

He stiffened. "Don't." His jaw clenched. "Even. Think. About. It."

For some reason his response only encouraged me more. It wasn't like I was going to get any answers from anyone else, and it was already hard staying away from him.

Staying away from the bad guy should never be a problem.

And yet it was mine.

If I closed my eyes I could see my dad's blood on his hands.

And yet I still wanted those hands on me.

Something was very wrong with me.

I groaned, grabbed the fork, and shoved another bite into my mouth, berating myself for being the worst sort of person.

For wanting his brand of danger.

And wishing that he would give in to my brand of temptation.

Chapter Eighteen

Vic

I'd managed to make it the entire day without seeing her. I watched. I definitely watched her. Hell, I knew when she grabbed a snack, bottle of water, when she used the restroom. And when she was in there a bit too long, I almost broke the door down only to hear the shower turn off.

I was in constant pain.

A shadow with a grimace.

Waiting in silence.

Watching.

Wishing.

It was pure hell.

Torture from the seventh circle.

And I endured. I had to. I had no choice but to protect her from everything. She had no idea how much she was worth. The mafia didn't do things by accident. It was no accident she had been asked to watch the children.

No accident she had been invited into this home, into our lives.

This was no summer job.

This was life or death.

And I hated that her world would eventually come crashing down around her, revealing that everything she thought she knew about herself was a lie.

And I would help deliver the crushing blow.

Fuck, I hated my life sometimes.

The bathroom door opened. She was wrapped in the shortest towel I'd ever seen in my entire life. Water droplets slid down her legs. I suppressed a groan and almost bit into my fist to keep from saying something that would destroy the oath I'd made.

I might be an assassin.

But I was still a man.

With wants, needs.

Damn, it was bad timing. I was ready to explode, and I had to babysit a woman who would tempt anyone—especially a man who'd been celibate for three years.

I squeezed my eyes shut so I wouldn't watch her ass as she walked back into my room and grabbed her clothes.

Slowly, I backed away, down the hall, and gazed out the large windows in the kitchen.

The gate was opening.

We weren't expecting visitors.

I breathed a sigh of relief when I noticed it was Chase pulling in. I grabbed my gun just in case, and opened the front door.

He parked.

Got out of his Maybach.

And strolled toward me like he had all the time in the world, like snipers weren't a real danger. He always believed that he was invincible. That nobody would dare hurt him considering the power he wielded within the Abandonato family, that paired with his scary political connections meant he could do anything he wanted and it would be covered up with roses.

Bleeding roses.

But roses all the same.

"Nice night, huh, Vic?" He grinned.

Swear the man was hell bent on torturing me ever since I'd followed him around his own house and accidentally seen his wife naked.

"Yup." I crossed my arms over my gun. "Did you need something?"

He shoved his hands in his pockets. "Some fresh air, you?"

I glared. "We don't do small talk, spit it out."

"Are you alone?" He tilted his head and peered around me like he could see into the house, into my room, see the towel drop from her naked body into a heap by her feet, see her breasts jiggle with each step toward her clothes, see her bend over and—"Vic?"

"No." I shook my head. "I mean yes."

What was the question?

"Have you thought about our little talk?"

"No." Yes. Every second of every day.

"Liar." He took a step toward me, then another. The maniac pulled out a knife and thumbed the blade, then charged me. I wasn't expecting it. I dropped my gun, my only weapon, and deflected the first stab with my right forearm before shoving him away and kicking him in the stomach.

He stumbled back, chest heaving, like he was enjoying the fight. What the hell was wrong with him?

He charged again, this time with his left hand, which oddly enough was better than his right. I ducked just as his right elbow came down on my back, his knee to my chin. I head butted him just in time for him to stumble back and laugh his ass off.

"What the hell, Chase!" I roared.

"Never say I didn't give you anything." Psychopath of the day tossed the knife in the air. "Better go clean up... In fact, I'm pretty sure there's a girl in there who would be pissed as hell to see you bleeding." A slow smile spread across his mouth. "Bet she'll attend to your wounds."

"What are you doing?" I growled.

He sobered. "What needs to be done. I'm pushing you. Because you'll martyr yourself for the family, because you're fucking losing your touch, because two weeks ago you would have at least gotten a few punches in. You're distracted. So I'm taking away the distraction. It will be our little secret." He shrugged. "Regain your focus before Nixon finds out, and let her help you with all the blood—"

"Damn it, Chase!"

His eyes narrowed before he chucked the knife directly at my chest. I barely moved out of the way in time.

"My point," he said just as the knife impaled itself in the door, "has been made..."

I jerked it out of the door and tossed it back to him. He caught it by the blade with two fingers and winked. "Have a good night."

"Fuck you!" I spat.

"Love you too!" He waved the knife, got in the car, and peeled out of the driveway just as the gate closed behind him.

I slammed the door even though he was gone.

At least it made me feel better.

Though my anger was simmering beneath the surface, bubbling, threatening to spill over and wreak havoc on my already shaky sanity.

"What's wrong?" Her voice.

That voice.

I gritted my teeth and turned.

She just had to be wearing white.

White shorts and a short white tank top.

A matching set.

Innocent.

Not yet stained with blood.

I opened my mouth and looked to the breakfast bar to keep myself from gawking at her. "Nothing, just Chase pissing me off again."

"Pissing you off so much that you decided to fight him?" Her voice was closer and then her hands were on my face.

No. It wasn't going to happen.

No.

No.

I clenched my fists.

Her thumbs rubbed down my cheeks. "Let's get you cleaned up."

"I'm fine."

"You're bleeding."

"I said I'm fine!" I yelled, pulling away because I had to, pulling away because my body craved that tenderness in her touch. Pulling away because my heart soared for more.

An oath.

I had taken an oath.

Nobody has to know.... Chase's voice was like a damn recorder in my head, only encouraging the things my body wanted, not reminding me why my body wasn't going to get it.

She jumped back, hurt etched on every pretty feature. Hurt I'd put there because my control was slipping, because one more touch would be my downfall.

I stomped over to the sink, wet a few paper towels, and dabbed my cheek. I winced. Damn Chase. I ran it under water again and then touched it to my eye. The burn was soothing.

It reminded me that I had a job.

It grounded me.

And then the sound of a bar stool getting plopped in front of me jolted me out of my pain.

The black leather bar stool was a foot away from me.

And Renee was climbing onto it like a toddler.

She got on her knees so we were at eye level.

I looked straight ahead, afraid to move.

Afraid to breathe.

Funny that fear should finally show itself in the form of a five foot six Sicilian woman hell bent on treating my wounds and not the two hundred twenty-five pound Russian I'd just shot in the head last week.

"Hold. Still." She grabbed the paper towel from my hand and started dabbing around my face, cleaning up the blood Chase had left there.

Tying my stomach into an insurmountable number of knots.

My heart pounded as she examined my face, cradling my chin with care as she turned it left and right. "Your eye will probably bruise a bit, but other than that…he lives!" She winked.

And I was tired.

So damn tired of doing the right thing.

My rigid body collapsed. I braced her hips to keep myself from falling to the floor and just begging her to let me hold her.

She ran her hands over my hair and tilted my chin up. "Should we go watch a movie or something?"

Close quarters, thighs touching, lights off. Sign me up. Not. And yet I found myself nodding.

And mentally shooting myself in the foot as I followed after her like a puppy starving for any morsel of attention sent my way.

Pathetic.

Desperate.

Needy.

I followed her into the theatre room.

I turned off the lights just as she grabbed the remote.

And it wasn't until the glow of the TV hit her face that I realized I'd made a grave mistake.

I'd put myself in a position of vulnerability with a woman who wanted to watch a scary movie.

Well, shit.

Chapter Nineteen

Vic

My palms were sweaty like I was on my first date.

We were five minutes in.

It was going to be a long night.

My phone buzzed.

Nixon: *Any surprises?*

I almost laughed out loud. Nope, just your cousin coming by to encourage me to sleep with the nanny to get it out of my system and pulling a knife so that she'd clean up the blood.

Nothing to see here!

Me: *We're secure.*

Nixon: *Good. I've been worried...*

I frowned.

Me: *Why?*

Nixon: *Because of who she is. She's a temptation to the Russians, a temptation to the cartels, she's a temptation to the De Langes. Part of me thinks it would be better to kill her than protect her.*

I clutched my phone so hard it almost splintered into a million pieces in my hand.

Me: *I've got this.*

Nixon: *I never said you didn't. I'm just saying we need to think about the families. They've already proven they are willing to attack on all sides for her blood.*

Me: *Her blood isn't theirs to take.*

Nixon: *I know. But we can only protect her for so long…*

Me: *Then we send her away. We give her to the FBI for witness protection.*

"No texting during movie night!" Renee laughed and tried to grab my phone. I jerked it away from her and stood.

"This isn't a game, Renee!" I yelled out of frustration, out of fear for her. "This is my job. This is your life. So if I have to answer a fucking text during a shit scary movie, I'm going to!"

Her face fell.

Shit!

I kept losing.

Doing everything wrong when I had all the right intentions.

"I'm sorry," I muttered. "I'm just under a lot of stress."

"Because of me?"

I gulped, staring at her throat instead of her mouth.

"You know, I think I'll just go to bed," she said in a soft voice, running more than walking out of the theatre room.

I did a small circle and threw my phone against the couch, only to pick it up and read the next text from Nixon.

Nixon: *You're right. We will deal with it day by day. For now, just make sure she's happy and she's safe.*

Happy?

Why did my mind immediately go to sleeping with her to make her happy?

As if that was going to fix everything and not make it worse?

Me: *On it.*

Nixon: *Have a good night.*

I almost laughed. A good night by myself, with a woman I couldn't touch? Not likely.

I hung my head and went searching for the woman who haunted me day and night.

I checked my room first.

Frowned when she wasn't there.

Then spent the next thirty minutes scared shitless as I scoured the entire house and finally ran outside.

I breathed a sigh of relief when she was sitting cross legged under one of the large oak trees in the backyard. Everything was fenced.

Didn't mean people couldn't still get in.

Especially if we could get out.

"What the hell!" I yelled, not realizing how scared I was until that moment, when I should have been able to control my emotions and couldn't.

She jolted a bit and turned. "What?"

"Never!" I shoved my gun back into my holster. "Never hide from me again. I don't care if you're pissed or sad or need space. I am your space. I'm your everything. You don't run away and pout, got it?"

Her eyes narrowed. "You made me upset, so I went for a walk around the prison yard!"

"You're so fucking spoiled!" Fear had me lashing out, that and the fact that I couldn't touch her, couldn't tell her why it was so important to keep her safe. "Look around you! Do you think that I want you to be stuck here? Do you think I like the fact that you can't go to school? I can't control this, but I can control being able to keep you safe. Let me do my job before you drive me insane!"

"I drive you insane, huh?"

"That's what you took from this heart to heart?"

"Oh, it was a heart to heart? Must have missed that with all the yelling." She crossed her arms and glared.

I dropped my head and ran my hand over the back of my neck. "I thought something happened to you."

"I was safe."

"I didn't know you were safe," I whispered, taking a cautious step toward her. "I need to know you're breathing… it drives me crazy when I can't see you."

She smiled up at me. "Because you like watching the nanny?"

"No." I shook my head and tilted her chin up. "I love watching the nanny."

I wasn't ready.

I wasn't prepared.

I was a soldier.

A killer.

It was unexpected for anyone to touch me. To seduce me.

So when she stood on her tiptoes, I didn't see it coming.

Maybe I didn't want to.

And when she pressed her mouth to mine.

I was still in such shock.

That I reacted.

Violently.

I shoved her against the tree and braced her hips with my hands. I rubbed small circles with my thumbs against those hips. I shamelessly devoured her lips, I swallowed each moan and lost myself.

I lost myself.

Or maybe—for the first time in years—I'd been found.

Chapter Twenty

Renee

I tasted his fear.

It mingled with his lust.

His desire.

I wanted him.

So I took him.

Because waiting for him to snap was like watching someone slowly burn from within until they lash out at everything around them. He felt the attraction. We were heat, we were untamed, we were greedy.

He reached for the front of my shirt and ripped it with his right hand. I gasped as he exposed my bra and then ripped that too, like I could go out and find another one just like it.

It would be easier if he was clumsy...

If he didn't know exactly what he was doing when his tongue slid past my lips and teased every inch of my mouth.

He knew.

He knew my body better than I did.

I arched into him wantonly.

He responded by lifting me with one arm and bracing me against the tree, running his wicked mouth down my neck and licking one nipple, only to go to the other like he'd been waiting to do it all day.

Each moan was swallowed by more deep kissing.

More, more, more.

"You're bad for me," he whispered against my neck. "I want you anyways."

"You're bad for me," I admitted. "I'll take you any way I can get."

He growled against my mouth, and the vibration of it sent shivers down my spine. Abruptly he pulled away.

I wanted to protest, to tell him not to run.

I didn't have to.

He threw me over his shoulder like I weighed nothing and carried me into the house, slamming the door behind him, locking it to keep bad guys out—or maybe to keep the baddest of them all...

In.

He tossed me onto the nearest couch and attacked. His mouth came down hard, next his body, until all I knew was him.

Vic's scent.

His taste.

The weight of him pressed against me.

I opened my mouth to him as he deepened the kiss. His rough hands cupped my breasts, weighing them, squeezing, as he sucked my tongue with his lips, bit down with his teeth.

Heart racing, I couldn't even form a logical thought beyond how good he tasted and how hot his skin was.

"This happens once." He pulled away abruptly. "Promise me."

I gulped.

"Renee." It was his tone, the sound of my name falling from his lips like he was tortured by my name—by me. I knew that kind of torture, I knew what it was like to kiss my enemy and want him in my bed.

To hate myself for wanting the murderer.

"Renee." His forehead touched mine, his chest heaved up and down, his eyes were fire, his touch almost painful as he gripped my shoulders. "Please."

"Yes," I whispered. "Only once—unless you initiate it."

He pressed an open-mouthed kiss to my neck. I bit down on my lower lip to keep from screaming his name when he sucked my collarbone between his lips and dragged his mouth along my chest, plunging a trail of desire all the way down the center of my body until he stopped at my belly button.

I waited.

He slowly lifted his head and smirked.

I almost orgasmed on the spot from that smirk.

He used both hands.

Both hands gripped my shorts.

Both hands tugged while he smirked.

His fingers dug into my skin as he pulled my shorts down my legs, taking my flimsy underwear right along with them.

His eyes locked on mine the entire time while his knuckles grazed my skin.

I gulped when he lifted my hips with both hands and in one swift motion pulled my entire body down the couch like he was ready for a feast.

I'd never seen this side of him.

It was predatory.

Focused.

Not on killing.

His job.

But on me.

I let out a yelp when he spread my legs open. There was no warning, no easing into things with him. It was action followed by more action, and God help me if he started to smirk again.

"What are you doing?" I asked.

"Did you need a play by play?" he asked, one eyebrow arched.

"Don't smirk at me." I somehow got the words out.

"Smirk?" He frowned. Thank God.

"Yeah." Basically stop being sexy and irresistible. Thanks.

He lowered his head between my legs. I could still see his eyes over my own nakedness. What was he waiting for? And why was I shamelessly just presenting myself to him?

At least the lights were low.

But not low enough that I couldn't see his every expression.

"Maybe..." His eyes never left mine. "Maybe I have something to be smug about."

"Oh yeah?" I couldn't calm my heart down. My legs started to tremble in anticipation, my thighs ready to squeeze. Every part of me was already primed and all he'd done was smirk while taking off my shorts.

I was in trouble.

"Yeah." He sobered, and I could swear time stood still as his lips parted into the most devious look I'd ever been given. He lowered his head. A startled gasp escaped my mouth when he didn't look away.

No, he watched me.

He. Watched. Me.

While he played.

While he moved his mouth over every inch of my core, while he pressed his fingers against every sensitive inch. His eyes never left mine.

I couldn't control the waves of pleasure or the way my body kept scooting closer to get more of him.

I closed my eyes for a second.

He stopped.

When I opened them he winked and the pleasure was back.

"Never..." His mouth vibrated against my thighs. "Never take your eyes away from me."

"Is that a fetish?" I tried teasing to lighten the moment, to give myself respite before I exploded.

"It's not a fetish to want to watch you come apart because of my mouth, because of my hands. It's not a fetish when a murderer wants to see what it looks like to create life—rather than death." His eyes locked onto mine with such intensity I couldn't breathe. "I see life in your eyes when I touch you."

"I don't know what to say," I whispered with a shaky breath.

"Ask me to touch you again. Ask me for more..." He moved until he was settled over me, my legs on either side of him. How was he even still dressed right now? "And say my name."

"Vic." My voice trembled as he stole kiss after kiss. "Vic."

He started to shake in my arms like hearing his name from my lips was better than the best sex.

And maybe—to someone like him—it was.

"Vic." I said his name again for me, not for him, so that I would remind my head and my heart that this was Vic. The same Vic who wasn't supposed to have sex, the same Vic who had taken an oath to protect the families, the same Vic who took an oath to protect me.

My father's murderer.

With shaking hands, I spread my palms across his chest and grabbed his gun from the holster and gently placed it on the floor. His breathing picked up when I pulled his black T-shirt over his head.

Nothing could have prepared me for the man underneath the shirt.

For the ink that covered every bare inch of skin on his chest and shoulders.

Or for the knife wounds those tattoos covered.

He stopped my exploring with a simple shake of his head, like my fingers touching his wounds just brought them back. I started unbuttoning his pants; he helped me pull them down. He was already straining toward me, every hard inch of him.

He squeezed his eyes shut when my hand grazed him, and then he was gripping my wrists with both hands. "This is going to be over way too soon."

"You're the one who said 'once,'" I reminded him.

His eyes flashed open. Maybe he was going to say something, maybe not, his lips parted and then he was kissing me—almost violently.

I liked it.

I liked his aggression.

The way he put his entire body and soul into his kiss—like he wouldn't get a second chance to do it again so he had to do it right the first and only time.

I couldn't keep up.

I kissed him back, bruising my mouth in the process. He fisted my hair in his right hand and cupped my ass with his left, giving me the perfect angle to feel his tip.

"Please," I begged. "Please, Vic."

He made an animalistic growl before driving into me so fast and hard that I almost stopped breathing.

He didn't move.

I cupped his face with both hands. He stared at me like I was his world—I'd never been looked at that way.

Tears filled my eyes as he lowered his head and pressed the softest of kisses against my mouth. He moved his hips and swallowed my moan as I clung to his body like a lifeline.

I squeezed the life out of him, felt my body collapsing around his like it was trying to hold on but couldn't last as long as it wanted.

"Renee." He rasped my name and I chose to believe it would forever be on his lips. "I've never...." He thrust so deep I cried out. The pleasure was too much. "Stay with me...." I nodded my head. "You're so close..." I gripped his shoulders digging my nails into his skin. "God, your thighs could kill a man..." He chuckled against my neck.

It was the most beautiful sound I'd ever heard in my entire life.

It was what sent me over the edge.

What set me free.

I found just as much pleasure in his laugh as I did in his body.

"Vic..." I touched his face. "Let go."

"Don't...I can't..." I could see the war on his face. But moments can't last forever, can they?

"Vic." My body pulsed and then he drove into me again, building me back up even after already coming back down. I was so shocked I couldn't control the release. He cried out—filled me with every part of him—and I greedily took it all—upset because I couldn't have more.

And when the aftershocks took me higher and higher, and when he adjusted inside me and I orgasmed again, I knew—I would never find the same pleasure in another man's arms.

Murderer...mine.

Chapter Twenty-One

Vic

I waited for the guilt to wash over me.

Instead, my brain was too pre-occupied with the fact that I had Nixon's naked nanny with me on their living room couch.

As far as bad decisions went...

This was up there with agreeing to take that damn oath and join the family business in the first place.

I wiped a hand down my face and turned toward Renee. She was all soft curves and light smiles.

It made my gut clench.

The fact that she even let me touch her, let alone... I reached out and thumbed her bottom lip and then cupped her by the neck and pulled her in for a kiss. I couldn't help myself. She tasted like life.

Made me feel less like death.

"You're smiling," she whispered in awe.

I frowned. "I am?"

She hit me lightly on the arm. "You were and then you ruined it."

I sighed and kissed her again then said, "Maybe you make me smile."

"Does that make me a devil charmer?" She scooted closer until I had no choice but to wrap my arms around her so we were chest to chest.

I kissed her forehead. "I guess that makes me the devil in this scenario."

She shrugged.

"Hah." I smiled again. It was alarming how hard it was to do, or at least how hard it used to be, but not with her in my arms. Never with her in my arms. She was the sunshine in my hell. "Are you..." I licked my lips. "Did you—"

"Stop." She covered my mouth with her hand. "I'm fantastic, though a little warning would be nice next time so I remember to breathe."

I frowned. "What do you mean remember to breathe?"

Her cheeks went bright pink. "You're not a small...man."

I barked out a rusty laugh. "I think that was a compliment?"

"Try not to let it get to your head." She tugged her lower lip between her teeth. God, I would do anything to taste her again, to never stop.

I eyed her mouth.

Then ran a hand down her backside.

"You're so smooth."

She shivered.

I would do anything for this woman.

I would protect her.

I would die for her.

I would...

I felt my entire body go tight. "Fuck."

"What?"

"Damn it!" I squeezed my eyes shut. "I'm sorry, Renee. Shit!" I couldn't even look at her.

"What? What's wrong?" She cupped my face.

I gritted my teeth. "I'm supposed to be protecting you and I didn't even think about protection! Fuck, I'll take you to the doctor and—"

"Vic?"

"What?" My stomach clenched.

"First, I'm not stupid—"

"I didn't say—"

She pressed a finger to my lips. Hell, was she shushing me? Was I smiling again? Damn it, the guys were going to suspect something if I didn't lock that shit down. Especially Nixon.

"Meaning," she continued, "even though you ooze sexuality and dominance—"

Now I was really smiling.

Her eyes narrowed. "I take back what I said about that smile."

"Too late." I chuckled as a dazed expression crossed her face. And then she was shaking her head.

"As I was saying…" Renee gulped and stared at my mouth in fascination. "I'm not stupid, I'm on the pill. And you said you hadn't been with anyone in three years, so…I figured I was okay."

Breath rushed out of my lungs. "You trust my word that much? What if I slipped during those three years? What if I slipped at the club the other night?"

"You wouldn't have slept with me then," she said in a quiet voice. "And men like you don't just slip…"

"And yet." I groaned into my hands. "I'm still sorry, Renee. I wasn't thinking."

"Good," she said softly. "You do enough thinking."

She pressed me onto my back and then laid her head on my chest. I played with her hair while she ran her nails up and down my sides. Something wet hit my chest. When I looked down two more tears rolled off her cheeks.

"Was he a bad man, my father?" Her voice was so quiet, so innocent. God, I shouldn't even be touching her.

"It was either we kill him without torture—or the Russians make it last for a few weeks… He was dirty because we asked him to be. He had to play both sides, and he knew if he ever got caught—" I swore. "He knew what would happen."

"And you—"

"Don't make me talk about this. Not when I'm holding his daughter—" I almost stuttered when I said daughter. "In my arms."

"Okay." She sniffled.

I hugged her tight and closed my eyes. "In three minutes…things go back to the way they were. They have to."

She clung to me tighter.

I fucking loved the way she plastered her body against mine as if to say *you can't make me.*

And I didn't want to.

But nobody could know.

Ever.

This wasn't in the oath I had taken.

And I wasn't good enough to be touching her, let alone sleeping with her.

I watched the grandfather clock in that room.

I watched it with a tight chest.

And slowly, as the seconds ticked by, I felt my body go rigid. I forced my smile away, purposefully shoved memories of her taste out of my brain, and clung to only one last thought before it chimed.

The way she said my name.

I was keeping that one.

Everything else...I would forget.

But I would remember the one time—someone made me feel less like a monster—more like a human, just by the way my name fell from her lips.

Chapter Twenty-Two

Renee

I slept alone.

But I knew he was watching.

Every night he watched.

Even after I was back at watching the kids in the early mornings, he never left my side.

And it was driving me insane.

It had been five days since the couch.

Five days of me walking in and out of that room, staring at the leather couch that he'd stripped me on. Where he'd made me scream, made me say his name.

"You okay?" A male voice jolted me out of my lust. I turned and smiled as Chase stared me down like he knew something I didn't. "You seem jumpy."

"Yeah, well, you guys are all packing." I shrugged just as Vic walked by.

Chase lowered his voice. "In more ways than one."

Searing heat flooded my cheeks.

Chase stretched his lips in a knowing grin. "That's what I thought."

Vic walked in front of the windows and then turned back to face us. I couldn't help my reaction any more than I could help breathing. His eyes darkened as he drank me in.

Next to me, Chase cleared his throat. "He watches you very...intensely."

"Maybe he's just good at his job."

"He's good at his job," Chase admitted. "When he's not distracted. And the shocking thing is, he hasn't been distracted for...five days or so, I would say?"

I clenched my fists and stared straight ahead.

"But who's counting?" Chase yawned. "You're always welcome in our house."

I whipped my head toward his. "What's that supposed to mean?"

"If Nixon ever decides to kick you out." He shrugged. "Our door is open."

"Why would he kick me out?"

Chase glanced over at Vic. "Why indeed?" He put a hand on my shoulder. "His acting's better than yours...reign it in, Nanny."

I pressed my palms to my hot cheeks. "Great. Just great."

Chase winked and sauntered off with a whistle as if he wasn't one of the most infuriating men I'd ever had the displeasure of meeting. He carried darkness with him, that one—then again, all of the men did. It was as if there was this giant chip on each of their shoulders that they kept there to purposefully punish themselves for the sins they'd committed.

I eyed the couch again then looked up.

Vic caught me.

His expression softened.

Great, now he was giving me looks of pity. The murderer!

I was fine.

Completely and totally fine.

I swallowed the tennis ball that had lodged its way into my throat and turned on my heel.

Family dinner be damned.

I knew they wanted to include me, but I needed to be alone. And if Chase said I wasn't able to reign it in? Well that wasn't a good sign, now was it?

"Where are you off to?" Nixon walked right in front of me.

Shit.

"I was, um, just going to wash up...for dinner," I lied.

He tilted his head. "Tex just went in there with Mo. Might be a few minutes, go use the kitchen."

I made a face.

Nixon cracked a smile. "Can't keep their hands off each other, and if they keep at it under my roof I'm going to be using Tex as target practice. I still don't see what my sister sees in him."

"Does Tex know this?"

"Oh, it's his favorite pastime, pissing me off. One day I'm going to take off a finger. I look forward to it with more enthusiasm than I should."

And with that, I was led into the kitchen, where I tried to wash my hands without thinking of Vic.

Where I tried calming my racing heart as people sat around the large table.

Seats were pulled out.

I waited.

Because bosses always sat first. Always in a way to protect the innocents around them. Each boss was assigned a family member to stand in front of if it came to a gun fight.

And since I was living under Nixon's roof, for whatever reason they still wouldn't tell me other than my only future was nannying their children and never getting an education, I swallowed the bitter pill and accepted it.

I was just about to grab a seat when Trace walked in and sat next to Nixon. I waited again. This time, in a blur of activity, people sat and I was the last one standing. Even Tex and Mo had made it back into the room.

One seat left.

Right next to Vic.

To make matters worse, Chase's smirk was not making me feel confident enough to make it through without blurting out that we'd had sex, thus getting Vic killed. An oath wasn't a small thing in the mafia and once you took one you basically had to see it through. Blood in, no out. You'd never be free of this. You'd have to die to be free. I sighed heavily.

At least Mo was to my left, Vic to my right.

I could do this.

"Chase, you say the blessing," Nixon demanded.

Chase's grin grew to epic proportions as he stared across at me. "Sure, I'll say an extra prayer God forgives us all for our sins…"

If I could kick him and not get shot at, I would.

I glared.

The normally gloomy assassin seemed thrilled to be teasing me, like it was the most entertainment he'd had in years.

His wife, Luc, elbowed him and shot me an apologetic glance.

The shocking part was that he actually listened.

And then wrapped a bulky arm around her and held her close.

His prayer was short.

I remembered nothing.

Even my name was fuzzy.

Because I could smell Vic.

And I wanted to take a bite.

Not of the food.

I was going to have to sit on my hands, wasn't I? That's what it was coming to.

Food was passed around.

It was taco night, which would have made my Sicilian grandmother roll over in her grave. According to my mother, one did not eat tacos during family dinner. But when you have toddlers you'll sacrifice a freaking cow just so they eat and stop trying to survive off air. Not like anyone at that table was going to get sainted anyway.

Tex grabbed a dinner roll and chucked it across the table. Dante caught it with one hand. "Too slow, old man."

Sergio laughed while Tex picked up a knife and pointed it in Sergio's direction. "Care to see if I miss?"

"Care to see if I poison your wine?" Sergio said it so calmly, but I knew he would do it just to see Tex crap his pants or do something equally embarrassing. These guys didn't understand the word boundaries. It was a family forged by blood, by loss, by so much love it almost seemed normal to bicker and pull weapons to prove your point. Family and God. They ruled with iron fists—they loved even harder than they killed.

I was surprised there were even knives allowed at the table after last month where the bosses got into a pissing match over tattoos.

"Renee." Nixon calling me out during dinner rarely happened. I didn't speak unless spoken to. "Your mother called."

"She did?" I exhaled in relief. "So I can go home soon?"

The table fell silent.

"Actually…" He cleared his throat. "She's decided to stay a bit longer in Vegas."

"How much longer?" My skin erupted in goose bumps. Something wasn't adding up. "Like a week?"

"Few months." He shrugged like it wasn't a big deal. "Besides, you're safer here."

I almost snorted. From who? What?

"Safer." I tasted the word and decided I hated it. "Safer from…?"

"People," Nixon answered in a bland tone. "People with guns who like to point them at other people."

"You just described every single person at this table!" I didn't mean to raise my voice. He must have been surprised because his eyebrows shot up.

He let out a sigh. "Trust us."

"Not to ruin family dinner, sir." I tried the respect card. "But why the hell aren't you telling me anything?"

"Because it would change nothing. Because knowledge is power. And because giving you that power will make you more of a target. You can't tell what you don't know."

I sighed. Hating that he had a point.

Hating that the guy was, what? Five years older than me with a lip ring and enough tattoos to blind a person, and he was lording over me like he had a right to.

Because he did.

Stupid mafia.

"So…" Chase interrupted. "Vic, bet you were bored the other night when everyone was gone and you were on babysitting duty." He popped some bread into his mouth and grinned at me.

Vic shrugged. "Nothing exciting."

"Really?" Chase piped up. "Not even the knife I threw at your face?"

"You missed." Vic shrugged. "Like I said, nothing exciting."

"Why'd you throw a knife at his face?" Luc smacked him in the arm.

Chase just shrugged. "Because I can?"

"Worst logic in the world," Mo muttered under her breath, earning a laugh from the other women at the table.

"But true." Chase picked up his taco. "Right, Vic?" He bit down. "You know what body part tacos remind me of?"

"Chase." Nixon's voice carried only exhaustion and a light warning tone.

Vic seemed completely unaffected.

And then I looked down at his side.

He was gripping his chair so tight his knuckles were white, his forearm muscles strained as he held on, blank expression in place.

I very lightly covered his one hand with mine, brief enough to be effective, not long enough to fulfill what I needed.

He exhaled like he'd needed my permission to relax.

And my hand buzzed with awareness the rest of the dinner.

Chapter Twenty-Three

Vic

I stared at myself in the bathroom mirror, gripping the sink with my hands so that I could squeeze something that wasn't Chase's throat. He knew I was ready to lose my struggle.

He saw it in my eyes.

Then brought attention to it.

Or maybe just saw the temptation was there to reach over and hold her hand.

Damn, the guy was infuriating!

I took a solid deep breath then went over to the door to jerk it open. Renee had her hand midair like she was ready to knock.

"Sorry," I croaked. "It's all yours."

"No, I mean, I just was going to shower really quick and…"

I closed my eyes and sighed. "Well, go for it." I sidestepped her only to have her try to sidestep me at the same time, making it look like we were doing this weird dance. Our clothes brushed each other.

"Fuck." I grabbed her wrist, holding her there.

Holding her where I could smell her.

I closed my eyes and inhaled, my eyes rolling to the back of my head when her scent washed over me. And still I grasped her by the wrist.

"Vic." I dropped her hand at the sound of Nixon's voice and stomped off in the direction of it.

"Yes?" He was in his office.

"Don't tell her, not yet. I know she can be…convincing." He gulped. "And she's innocent enough to want to share details with, but don't get so close to her that you forget your purpose in watching her."

"To keep her alive." I nodded.

"For her betrothed back in Sicily." He dug the knife deeper, twisted, twisted, and twisted some more.

"Yes," I bit out. "For her betrothed."

"Good."

I was dismissed, except… "Nixon? Were you going to give her her own room?"

"She's safer in yours by location alone…unless it's becoming a problem…watching her?"

Never. "I've got it handled."

"All right then."

I berated myself the entire walk back to my room and again when I was just in time to see her yawn and stretch her arms over her head. That flimsy white tank top was fooling nobody. How was that even considered a shirt? I walked into the room, plopped down on my usual stalker chair, and reached for a book. Staring at her would make me rip her clothes off with my teeth with Nixon a few feet away.

I cleared my throat.

Twice.

And then looked up when the light didn't turn off.

She was staring at me.

"What are you doing?" I closed the book.

She lifted a shoulder in half a shrug. "Watching the bodyguard."

My lips twitched. "Must be boring."

"He's really pretty to look at," she whispered. "Sharpest jaw I've ever seen, intense blue eyes that cut right through a person—muscles sculpted all around his rock-hard body—it's better than Kardashians, that's for sure."

"Wow, color me relieved," I deadpanned.

She just smiled brighter, forcing me to experience her joy even when I was hell-bent on ignoring it.

She was a flame, wasn't she?

And I was a fucking stupid moth.

"Did you need me to get the light?" I stood and walked over to the door, pausing only a second before flipping it off. My hand hovered near the lock on the door.

Temptation pulsed and pounded; it begged, it clawed at me, screamed. I ignored it and took a seat, now blanketed in darkness, my book forgotten.

"Hey, Vic?" Renee called out into the darkness.

"Yeah?"

"Are you watching?"

Those three words.

Would be my downfall.

I could feel it in the air as I locked eyes on her and watched her dip her fingers beneath the covers. I sucked in a breath, unable to look away.

Her hips lifted off the bed.

And then she was pulling shorts out from under the covers and tossing them onto the floor.

"Are you watching?" she repeated.

I was paralyzed.

Frozen.

Aroused.

She threw the covers off her body and ran her hands down her breasts as they strained against the white tank.

She watched me while I watched her.

And then she slid one hand down her stomach, lower, lower.

I don't remember moving.

I was in the chair.

And then my mouth was on hers in a punishing kiss. "Never." I squeezed her ass. "Touch yourself without letting me touch you first."

"Greedy?" she asked.

"Fuck yes." I flipped her onto her stomach and ran my hands down the curves of her body. I could worship her like this. "You're so beautiful."

She was meant for someone else.

Nixon could walk in.

I'd made an oath.

I batted the thoughts out of my head. "So. Perfect."

"Take your clothes off." She didn't have to beg me, I was already sliding my pants down my hips, already pulsing with this aggressive need to claim her in my bed, against my mattress.

Mine.

I flipped her back over onto her back and hooked her knees over my shoulders, then clapped a hand over her mouth. "Shhhhh."

She nodded. Her eyes wild.

I entered her in one smooth thrust that had her biting my hand. I didn't pull away. Let her bite, let her draw blood, just don't let her scream.

Even though it would be the most beautiful noise in the world, her screaming my name while she climaxed.

That wasn't our future, was it?

My body shuddered as she spasmed around me. Fuck, I could feel her heartbeat with each pulse, with each thrust.

It screamed my name when her words couldn't.

And I responded in the only way I knew how.

I rose over her as she relentlessly matched my rhythm with her hips. There was nothing careful about what we were doing, nothing slow.

We weren't given that luxury, were we?

All the reasons we couldn't be together tumbled into oblivion the minute she'd touched herself, the minute she told me she was watching.

I leaned down and moaned against her neck, my lips met hers in a frenzied kiss. I slowed my thrusts to make the moment longer, to wish it into an eternal forever I knew would never exist except in those times when she was mine, when I was inside her, when my name beat against her heart.

She clawed at me like she needed me closer. I slid in deeper, earning another gasp from her before she found her release.

I wasn't far behind.

We stared at one another, chests heaving.

The smell of sex in the air.

Things left unsaid between us.

I kissed her forehead.

Tears filled her eyes.

I kissed each cheek. And then I tucked her into bed as tightly as I could. I felt older than my thirty years as I walked over to the chair, sat, and did my job.

"Will you be watching, Vic?" she asked in a sleepy voice.

"Always," I croaked, unable to keep the emotion from my voice.

"Maybe one day you won't have to."

"Maybe," I said, giving her false hope. Making her think it was possible that the story could end differently if she just believed hard enough. I'd give her the lie any day of the week, because the truth would destroy her.

The truth of her birth.
The truth of her past.
Her future.
I was nowhere in any of those truths.
So I would lie.
Because at least in the lie—she would be in my arms.

Chapter Twenty-Four

Renee

It was wrong.

I didn't care.

In fact I was beyond caring.

Not to the point where I wanted to expose us and get Vic in trouble, but to the point where my need for him trumped all reason and logic. It made me justify my actions in the worst way.

My day went by so slow I thought I was going to lose my mind, and as slow days went—the kids were little tyrants, so by the time dinner rolled around I just wanted to go to bed early with a movie.

When I walked into Vic's bedroom there was a candle lit and a plate of food waiting on the nightstand.

Next to that was my open laptop with Netflix already on the webpage.

I smiled.

And then the smile fell.

This wasn't a date.

He wasn't staying with me.

This was him doing something nice.

Because he'd taken an oath. He would never be by my side, and part of me understood why. I just didn't want to accept any of it.

I crawled onto his bed and started to eat just as someone stopped in the middle of the doorway.

"Vic." I breathed his name like it was my favorite word, and maybe it was. "Thank you for the food and movie…" I shrugged. "I was exhausted today."

He smirked. *Damn it, stop smirking if you want me to keep you from getting shot!*

"I know." He sat back down in his usual chair. "I think the whole 'I'm going to sell you at Walmart if you don't start listening' was my first clue."

I laughed. "Serena's such a diva!"

"Hey, she wanted her crown, no reason why you couldn't just get into a car and drive all the way into town and find her a leopard one."

I rolled my eyes. "I was never that much of a handful."

"Somehow, I doubt that. But whatever helps you sleep at night, princess." His face went from happy to sad like someone had just let the light out of his body.

"What's wrong?"

He shrugged. "You're not the only one who's exhausted. I was the one who chased Junior for at least five miles while you and Serena had your talk."

"You're six times his size, I'm sure you'll make it."

His smile was back. "Do you need anything else?"

"You," I blurted. And then instantly regretted it when his face fell. "What? Not on the menu?"

He didn't move from his spot in the chair. His fingers dug into the leather. "I don't think it would be wise since I tend to lose my head when I'm with you—and since Nixon would remove it from my body if he witnesses it."

I sighed. "I know. Sorry…"

"Don't be sorry. I want to be wanted."

I felt my entire body soften and lean toward him. "I don't think that's something you ever need to worry about where I'm concerned."

"Careful…" he whispered. "You're going to get me to break my oath a third time."

"Eh, what's one more time?"

"And I'm the bad guy." He shook his head and then crooked his finger at me. I made my way over to him and straddled his lap while he gripped my hips. "I want you every second of every day. I can't stop."

"I never asked you to stop."

"It would be wise to stop."

"It would be wise to kiss me—"

His mouth devoured my next sentence as his hands tangled in my hair. I slid my tongue past his lower lip, tasting wine on his tongue.

"Vic?" Chase called out his name loud enough that we both jumped apart. I sat on my bed and grabbed my dinner plate, eating vigorously while Vic grabbed the book sitting on the nightstand. Chase poked his head in the room and sighed. "You're lucky...this time."

"What do you mean?" I asked innocently.

Chase rolled his eyes. "It smells like horny high schoolers in here, all right? Rein it in or at least wait until Nixon's sleeping..." He eyed Vic. "He wants to see you."

"Again?" Vic blurted.

Again? What did he mean again? The food seemed to go dry in my mouth as Vic slowly rose from his seat and made his way out of the room past Chase and down the hall.

I stared down at my plate, feigning interest in the green broccoli sitting on it.

Chase cleared his throat.

"What?" I didn't look up.

"I encouraged this...in the beginning." His voice carried a hard edge that had goose bumps erupting up and down my body. "I misread the situation. I assumed he needed a bit of release so he could do his job."

My stomach clenched. "Oh."

"I'm rarely wrong," Chase admitted. "And for that...I'm sorry, more than you'll ever know."

"Sorry?" I finally looked up into his blue eyes. The haunted look was back, like he was trying to keep the demons away but too tired to fight them tonight. "What exactly are you sorry for?"

"Helping break your heart." He licked his lips, nodded at me once, then walked off.

Sickness wrapped itself around my insides. I crossed my arms and closed myself off to the world. I wasn't hungry. I wasn't tired. I was just...confused.

And maybe a lot afraid.

Afraid of the heaviness in Chase's words.

Afraid of the fact that Nixon kept pulling Vic into his office.

I shuddered.

"Everything all right?" Nixon poked his head in the doorway.

"Um, yeah." I frowned. "Are you watching me tonight?"

He smiled. "No. Vic had to run an errand, but he'll be back in a bit. He said he brought you dinner and a movie…and I'm sorry Serena decided that today of all days we should crown her as princess of the family."

I smiled at that. "Yeah, well, every little girl wants to be a princess, right?"

He sobered. "Some already are."

I frowned and then laughed. "Yeah, maybe in Europe."

He was silent, his eyes averted as he asked, "Renee, do you like it here?"

"In this house? This family?"

"Yes."

I sighed. "There's nowhere I'd rather be. You know, except my own home… The only thing missing is all the information you refuse to give me."

He nodded. "Soon."

"How soon?"

"Too soon," he fired back. "And yet, not soon enough."

"Vague, Nixon. Very vague."

"Relax." He ignored my jab and shut the bedroom door.

I tried to concentrate on the movie but my thoughts kept going back to Vic. What errand had Nixon sent him on? And why couldn't he send someone else?

I stared at the clock. Six at night.

I would wait for him.

I needed him.

I needed him more than he would ever know.

Chapter Twenty-Five

Vic

I pulled up to the club again. Hating that I was the one getting sent. I needed to face the facts, the more I fell for Renee, the more I hated my job. The more I wanted to say fuck it all and run away with her.

Leave it all behind.

No wonder I'd taken an oath.

Maybe Nixon knew that my one personality flaw was that I loved too much. Loved too hard. I didn't know how to go in halfway. So when I saw something I wanted, I dove head first with my heart and left my brain behind.

I nodded to security and the rope was pulled back. I walked through the club and all its patrons, with their masks and capes, their anonymous trysts and thick makeup.

The dance floor wasn't as crowded as last time.

Andrei nodded down at me and gave me his back.

Shit. *He* was here.

I slowly climbed the stairs, trying to bide my time before I had to see his face, before I had to hear the possessive words fall from his mouth. Music pumped around me. It was alive, and free. While I was walking toward a prison. Toward my end. I could have sworn my heart slowed to a depressed surly beat.

Andrei handed me a glass of whiskey, but I was going to need more than one glass after tonight. I took my seat and placed my Glock on the table pointed at Angelo Sinacore.

He wasn't the boss of the Sinacore family. He was a spoiled second son who was still trying to prove to his own family to get made.

The only power he had came from who his father was.

The only money he had was saved in a trust for when he turned twenty-eight.

He was wearing a gray suit with a red tie, fucking aviator glasses in the dark, and his greasy long black hair draped past his ears. He was everything that was wrong with the mafia.

He was wrong.

All wrong.

He was also considered royalty in Sicily.

"You have the girl?" He grinned, his straight white teeth flashed like he was ready to take a bite out of her.

"We do." I nodded.

"Thank you." He leaned forward, clasping his hands together. "For taking care of her until we could make arrangements. It is a rare find."

"You speak of her as if she's a lost artifact." Andrei snorted in disgust.

For once I agreed with the Russian.

"Ah, but to her country she is, dirty Russian."

Andrei smiled, but his posture stiffened, his eyes zeroed in on my gun. *I wish.*

"You will bring me to her." Angelo leaned back and pulled out a cigar.

"The arrangement for exchange is tomorrow evening," I said in the most bored voice I could muster. "You will wait a day. It states so in the contract, we wouldn't want that to be void."

His eyes narrowed a bit and then one nod and a dismissal with his hand. I had more money than his entire trust fund, more guns hidden on my body than he probably had in his entire arsenal.

He'd never seen the bloody side of the mafia.

Only the money.

The power.

You don't deserve something you never have to fight for. And he hadn't fought one day of his entire existence.

I stood.

"One more thing…" Angelo leaned forward. "Is she…a virgin?"

I clenched my fists, and lost complete control.

Andrei intercepted my right hand just in time and laughed. "Angelo, now you sound Russian."

Angelo looked insulted.

"Why does it matter if she's a virgin?"

"It matters because she will be marrying me, and I want to make sure she hasn't been spreading her legs for Russian scum."

Andrei's smile fell. "Watch it. This is still my club. I have at least seven guns trained on you, and I wouldn't push the Cosa Nostra's best assassin when he's having a shitty day."

Angelo adjusted his tie. "I can be curious about my future wife."

I took a deep breath. "We haven't conducted a medical exam. She's been in the house ever since we had final documents on her birthright."

"Ah." Angelo nodded. "And Nixon does not allow such things under his roof. I feel better now. I think…" He winked at us. "I'll go find myself someone for my last night of bachelorhood."

He sauntered off.

I imagined shooting his head off his body.

It didn't help.

"So…" Andrei shoved his hands in his pockets. "Exactly how many times have you broken your oath to the Family?"

I stared straight ahead. Andrei always was a mind reader. Or maybe my reaction was too violent—I never reacted. Angelo didn't know that. Andrei did.

"Once," I whispered. "With her."

"Oh, I know who you were with." Andrei chuckled. "My question is more of a…did our little assassin accidentally sleep with the nanny and then apologize for it…or has he been…doing more?"

"What do you want?" I clenched my teeth. Rage settled over my body like a hot blanket.

"Interesting." He crossed his arms. "Very interesting. I imagine Nixon has no idea, too focused on his family. But the other men, they know. Trust me."

"Chase encouraged…he baited…Chase is the devil," I finally admitted.

"That, he is." Andrei nodded encouragingly. "Was one woman truly worth death, Vic?"

I lifted my head and stared him down. "When that one woman is the only thing that makes you feel alive in this shit universe. Yes. It was worth it. It is worth it."

"And when you die?"

"Still worth it."

"And when she suffers because of it?"

I squeezed my eyes shut. "Protect her when I can't."

Andrei swore. "Well, that escalated quickly." A single nod. "I give you my word."

He held out his forearm. I grabbed it at the elbow and squeezed.

He leaned in as our foreheads touched briefly, his hand on the back of my neck.

"It is done," he said.

I grabbed my knife from my pocket and slit the palm of my hand. He held out his hand and did the same.

"Sangue en, non Fuori," we said in unison and parted ways. His eyes saw secrets, they fed off pain.

Andrei was one person I wanted in my corner because when it came down to it, he would burn the entire world to get his way and protect those he called friends—he would kill his loved ones in cold blood, he would laugh as he sent their souls to hell.

The enemy of my supposed ally will always be my strongest friend.

We needed more men willing to do the hard thing in this world, men who had not gone soft.

A few dancers made their way to the VIP section and wrapped their arms around him.

He didn't stiffen, just turned his head to the right and kissed one of them while the other sucked on his neck.

Anyone watching would see pleasure.

Anyone but someone who knew what it was like to live in a state of constant pain, of constant want—knowing that you'll never have your heart's desire.

His eyes were indifferent.

His body language relaxed.

Except for his one tell.

His right foot tapped impatiently on the floor, and his eyes, for one brief moment flashed to the cages on the stage, and burned black.

I didn't turn to see who held his interest.

Because I didn't want to feel guilty when she was sold.

Andrei was in deep.

The only way out was death or bringing the rings down.

Which was why he chose to play the part of the bad guy—it came so naturally, why not give in to sin?

So he did.

And I wondered, as I walked out of his club, how long it would be before he just let it consume all the light he had left.

Chapter Twenty-Six

Renee

He never came.

I waited for him.

And he never came.

I finally fell asleep with the lights on, staring at his chair and wondering what was so important that he couldn't come in and at least let me know he was okay.

It was around three a.m. when I finally got up and flipped the light off only to see light in the hallway and a person's shoes in front of my door. I frowned down at the small crack and then felt ready to pummel the life out of him for not telling me he was okay.

I jerked the door open.

Vic didn't move.

He stared straight ahead like the wall was talking to him.

So I smacked him in the back. "You could have told me you were alive!"

He didn't turn around, just hung his head. "I'm alive."

"Well, I know that...now." I crossed my arms. "I waited for you..."

He let out a sigh. I couldn't tell if it was irritated or sad, maybe a mixture of both? "I apologize for your loss of sleep."

Had I heard him right? "Um, what? You apologize for my lack of sleep? Are you a robot?" I smacked him again. "And turn around when we're talking!"

Slowly, he turned and faced me. His eyes were dark, his face hardened like he'd just been told that everyone he loved was going to die—and it was his fault.

"Wh-what happened?" I reached for his face, but he pulled away. "Vic…"

He made his hands into fists and pressed them against the wall like he was aiming to punch straight through. "You should sleep."

"I should also probably stop smacking a guy who's carrying multiple knives and guns, but I can't seem to help myself," I said softly.

He closed his eyes like he was in pain.

"Vic." I touched him lightly on the arm.

He hissed, then bit down on his lower lip. My eyes traveled up his arm. White gauze was wrapped around his hand and tied on the back.

"What's that?" I reached for his hand.

He jerked it away. "Renee." His tone was stern. "Go to bed. Now."

"Fine, I'll just go tell Nixon I know what your face looks like when you—" He slammed a hand over my mouth so fast I almost stumbled backwards. And then he was pulling me into the bedroom and shutting the door, locking us in.

Keeping them out.

My chest heaved as his gruff voice sounded in my ear. "You wouldn't."

"I wouldn't," I admitted. "But you weren't playing fair, so I upped the stakes."

"Fuck the stakes." He laughed sourly. "The game's already over, Renee."

"It's not a game."

"Then why does it feel like it?" He released me and then spun around and ran his hands over his head. Footsteps sounded in the hall. We both froze, not that we were doing anything wrong. Slowly Vic made his way to the chair and sat just as someone stopped in front of the door and then kept walking.

I exhaled as he leaned back in the chair and stared me down. He didn't even blink.

"How did you hurt your hand?" I pointed and then crossed the floor to where he was and sat on the bed.

He leaned forward, putting his knees on his elbows. "If I said I hurt it on purpose in order to protect someone I love—would you believe me?"

"Yes," I whispered, suddenly feeling like this was bigger than us, bigger than something I could even possibly try to understand. "I would…" I licked my dry lips. "Is that what happened?"

"No. Actually, I just slit my own palm with my knife in an effort to confuse the guy holding a gun to my head. It gave me enough time to disarm him and save the world." His lips twitched.

"Ass!" I threw a pillow at him. He didn't even deflect it, so I tried hitting him again then ended up being grabbed midair since I was still holding the pillow. I wrapped my legs around him, dropped the pillow, and braced myself against his body.

His eyes fell to my mouth.

"Why do you look angry and sad?" I asked, cupping his face with my hands while he braced my body with his. "Is there anything I can do to make you laugh?"

"I rarely laugh."

"Your laugh makes me feel real joy," I admitted.

His face fell. "You deserve all the joy in the world, Renee."

"Then stop being so stingy with it." I winked, meeting him halfway for a kiss. He didn't kiss me back.

I tilted my head. "Do you not…I mean, is this about…" I couldn't even get the words out before his mouth came crashing down on mine with such ferocity I almost fell out of his arms. He angled his head to deepen the kiss. I moaned when I fell back onto the mattress. His fingers clawed for my tank as he pulled it over my head and feasted his eyes on me. I could see the indecision on his face.

So I leaned up on my elbows and started pulling off his pants, making the decision for him. The bold caress of his tongue only encouraged me more as his hands closed around my breasts, coaxing me with a promise for more. He dragged his mouth from mine when I tugged his jeans down, exposing his hard length. I could have sworn it was throbbing or maybe that was me, I was in physical pain for wanting him so desperately. His body surged toward mine and then with a deep primitive growl, he drove into me as I clutched a fistful of his shirt and held on. An aching tension built between us as a frenzied look crossed his face. I pulled back, cupping his cheeks, slowing the process down. He pulled my hands away and then flipped our positions and pulled me back onto him so I could ride him.

"Renee?"

"Yes." I slid onto him and couldn't help but squeeze my eyes shut as a spasm of pleasure hit. I was breathtakingly aware of every movement as he pressed his large hands into my hips and sped up my rhythm.

"Say my name."

I leaned down and whispered across his lips. "Vic."

His body convulsed beneath mine as every muscle went taut.

"Vic." I said it again because I liked hearing it, I liked saying it. I could feel my blood humming in my veins as I took him deep, kept him there. Promised to never let him go. "You're mine, Vic."

His glassy eyes looked into my soul. "I'll always be yours."

And then he was relentlessly moving with me, pushing us toward completion when I didn't want to be anywhere but there in that moment with him inside me, telling me that we belonged to each other.

Pain crossed his face when his restraint snapped. I sighed in ecstasy when I felt him inside me, truly making me a part of him. I shuddered limp against his body and prayed he'd stay that way so I could feel our skin pressed against each other.

But he didn't.

He slowly lifted me off of him, grabbed my clothes, helped me dress, wordlessly tucked me into bed and pulled the duvet over my body.

"You're not staying?" My chest felt tight, and I had no idea why, why was I sad? Why was he sad?

"Not tonight" was all he said as he leaned down and brushed a soft kiss across my cheek. "But I'll be watching."

"My protector," I whispered, not realizing I was as tired as I really was. He made it to the door and watched me like he promised for a few seconds. My heavy eyelids finally closed just as I could have sworn I heard the words "forgive me" fall from his lips.

Chapter Twenty-Seven

Vic

I didn't sleep.

I would sleep when she was gone.

When I could rage in the privacy of my own room, when I could torture myself with sheets I would never wash.

With memories I would never forget.

"Don't take this the wrong way," Chase said as he walked into the room for dinner the next night. "But you look like shit."

"Don't take this the wrong way." I flipped him off and jerked out a chair so I could at least sit and not pace the hallway she was supposed to be walking down any minute.

The exchange was taking place at nine.

Fuck.

I had three hours left.

Three. Hours.

I would not survive this sort of loss.

I had never realized.

And now I did.

A panicked feeling washed over me, making my entire body want to bolt from the room, throw her over my shoulder, and catch the first flight to Mexico.

Let them chase us.

I'd kill them all.

Over her.

For her.

For us.

I ran my hands through my hair and down my face, realizing I hadn't shaved in a day and probably looked a second away from snapping.

Chase sat down across from me and let out a long sigh. "I didn't know."

"Know?"

"That you loved her. I didn't know this was more than sex. Had I known, I would have done the right thing and locked you in the basement."

I snorted. "You think that would have kept me away?"

"Shit, that's…" He poured himself a glass of wine. "What if we tell Nixon? See if there's a way out of this where we don't have to go to war with the Sicilian families? She's over eighteen, she can have a say."

I smiled sadly. "You of all people should know that we rarely get a say in this life."

His demeanor darkened. "Yeah, well…"

"Thank you, though."

"Don't thank me for helping ruin you—I wouldn't wish the loss of love on anyone, not even my greatest enemy. This isn't fair to her, we both know that. But her one life keeps us at peace with the Sicilians, it keeps her safe from the Russians and the De Langes." He lifted the wine to his lips. I could tell he was far away again, thinking of the past. Worrying over the future as any person did when they had a family.

A family.

I almost laughed.

I thought I knew what family was.

Until her.

And now I realized the family I'd always had was missing a pivotal piece, a partner.

We didn't speak anymore to one another. He was lost in the past.

And I was mourning my future.

My family all slowly trickled in.

Things got louder and louder until the noise just consumed me. And finally Renee made it down the hall and sat at the table across from me.

And then, she lifted her eyes and smiled.

At me.

Her father's murderer.

She gave me something in that smile.

She gave me hope that it wasn't going to be the last time I saw her smile.

She made me feel in that smile.

She started a war with that smile.

I stood abruptly. "I need some air."

I stomped my way down the hall and jerked open the first door that wasn't locked.

The bathroom.

I opened up the windows and leaned out, inhaling, exhaling. Twisting all possible outcomes until the problem got harder rather than unraveled.

A knock sounded.

"Go away."

The doorknob turned. I should have locked the door.

"I said—"

Renee stood there, her back against the door, her face full of longing. She took two steps toward me. They were small, tentative, the way you approach a wild animal.

"We can't." I squeezed my eyes shut. I couldn't look at her and deny her anything.

"Open your eyes." She gripped my biceps with her hands. Slowly, I opened my eyes and stared down at her beauty, something I would remember when I was old and gray if I ever made it that long. The way her eyes sparkled like she had a secret she wanted to share. "Let me love you."

I recklessly lowered my mouth to hers. I tasted my sin on her lips, I tasted my greatest blessing and greatest curse as our bodies brushed against one another. And when I lifted her onto the counter and cupped the back of her head, pulling her closer, drugging myself with her kiss, with her touch, I hated everyone and everything that would take her from me.

Her softness, her joy stirred something fierce within me, something uncontrollable. We were fire, we were burning each other alive. She had no idea what the next few hours held.

But I could give her pleasure so that when she met the devil—she'd at least know that heaven still existed.

I swiftly dealt with her leggings, rolling them down her legs carefully so she didn't return to dinner looking like I'd just been with her. I even kept myself from pulling at her hair, from sniffing it between my fingers and mussing it just because it made her look wild and sexy.

I teased her lips apart with my tongue while she clung to me with tears in her eyes, like she knew this was goodbye.

Like she knew this would not happen again.

Maybe it was in the tenderness of my kiss.

Maybe it was in the devastation I refused to hide.

I felt broken, and she wasn't even gone.

I felt dead, and she was still alive.

Reason quickly tumbled into oblivion as she reached into my pants, pumping me with one hand while tugging down my jeans with the other.

She slid her hand along my length.

I braced myself against her and then pulled her forward, teasing her entrance with little grazes before she devoured my next kiss with such intensity that I lost all concentration and filled her to the hilt.

"Why does this feel like the end?" Her body moved so effortlessly with mine, like we were made for this, for each other, nobody else.

"You will always have protection." I avoided her question. "And you'll always have this." I grabbed her hand and pressed it to my chest so she could feel the way my heart beat for her, each thump like a song in her honor. My blood rushed through my veins for her and only her.

A surge of possession washed over me when she grabbed my hand and placed it on her chest. "And you'll always have this."

Our foreheads touched as I pressed into her, taking my fill. Tension built between us as her body convulsed around me. I soaked in the way her head fell back, the way her lips parted in pleasure.

I memorized it.

And then I slid in one last time.

Pleasure rocked my body so intensely that I had to hold on to her to keep myself from shoving her body into the mirror behind her.

Tears filled her eyes as she cupped my face.

I tried to look away.

"Tell me." She whispered. "Now."

I opened my mouth, just as the bathroom door burst open.

I shoved her behind me.

Nixon looked between us and whispered in a gravelly voice, "Put your clothes on. You have three minutes to make your way to the kitchen."

The door slammed.

Renee covered her mouth with her hands then pressed them to her chest. "Is he going to kill me?"

"No. You're too valuable… Me, on the other hand…" I sighed.

Chapter Twenty-Eight

Renee

I wanted to reach for his hand as we walked back into the kitchen, but I wasn't sure if that would just be like dumping gasoline on an already out-of-control bonfire.

Everyone was silent.

I was so embarrassed I wanted to cry.

Embarrassed that they probably knew what we were doing.

Embarrassed that I'd done it in my employers' house.

And terrified for Vic.

What was I thinking?

Oh right, that I had found my one.

The one.

That I found someone who saw me, who got me, who made me feel alive, who made me feel both scared and secure. I'd found him. And when you find something that incredible...

You risk it all.

Without any thought of the consequences.

He'd warned me.

I hung my head only to have Luciana walk over to me and put an arm around my body like she was trying to protect me from Nixon. And slowly, one by one, the wives walked to my side and stood.

I wasn't comforted.

Because why was it necessary for all of them to be standing there? Mo, Trace, Bee, Val, Luc, El?

Nixon paced in front of Vic. And to his credit Vic just stared straight ahead, bulky arms at his sides.

"Who knew?" Nixon stopped in front of Vic. He still said nothing.

Chase cursed. "Nixon, no offense, but how didn't you know?"

Nixon could have incinerated someone with that glare.

Tex looked away. Sergio stared down at his feet. And Phoenix stared at Nixon with an indifferent look that I couldn't quite place while Dante made his way next to Vic's side and stood.

"Hold out your hand," Nixon demanded in a harsh voice.

Vic held out his hand. Dante handed Nixon a sharp dagger.

I watched in horror as Nixon dug the knife into the top of Vic's hand and started etching out the different names that he'd sworn to protect. Vic shook but made no noise.

Tears streamed down my face. "Stop! Stop it!"

Nixon didn't stop.

"STOP!" I roared. "You're a monster!"

His lips moved like he was ready to smile. "*I'm* a monster? Pretty sure you were fucking a monster. We're all monsters, Renee. We just conceal our demons in different ways."

I wiped my wet cheeks. "It was me. I seduced him."

Nixon let out a sigh of disbelief. "So you seduced him and what? He finally gave in? Vic is one of the strongest men I know. People like Vic don't give in to seduction unless they're already there."

I let out a gasp.

"And you..." He eyed Vic with so much anger I wanted to run over and protect him, stand in front of him and hold my hands out so that the daggers were thrown at me, not him. Anyone but him. "What do you have to say for yourself?"

"Nothing," Vic said in a solid voice. "I can't defend my actions, nor will I apologize for them."

Nixon threw a right hook.

Vic didn't deflect.

I watched as Nixon hit him again and again until he collapsed to the floor, and then Nixon's boot collided with Vic's ribs. And still Vic didn't deflect. He took his punishment.

"Nixon." Chase stepped forward. "You may as well punish me too. Vic confided in me, I helped hurry this along...I didn't...I thought it was just... a sex thing."

"Does this look like a fucking sex thing?" Nixon roared, pointing down at Vic. "He loves her!"

Hot wet tears trickled down my cheeks past my lips.

"I could forgive a lot of things..." Nixon stopped kicking Vic and leaned down so they were at eye level. "I could even forgive an indiscretion. But this? You swore an oath to us—to not just be celibate, but how can you protect any of the children, the women in the Family when your sole focus will always be on your own?"

"I can't." Vic's voice trembled.

"I know." Nixon shook his head and then stood and kicked the cabinets. "You know the Sinacore family is expecting her in less than three hours. She's going to be sobbing on a plane over the man she loves rather than talking with the one she's betrothed to!"

I swayed on my feet as my heart caught in my throat. "Betrothed?"

All eyes fell to me. I shook my head and narrowed my gaze on Vic. Blood caked his face, but I could still see the guilt all the same.

"Betrothed," I said again. "What the hell do you mean betrothed? Why would you marry me off in the first place? Is this because of my father? What he did?"

"Renee..." Nixon's expression softened.

"I'm not marrying a stranger!"

"Renee!" Nixon barked. "You're fucking royalty. You'll marry who we tell you to marry because you're the last in line! Your father died getting this information to us! He died trying to protect you. Your mother is in a safe house until this deal is finished!"

"Wh-what?"

He sighed and ran a hand through his hair. "The Sinacore family is one of the oldest families in Sicily. They were at one time considered royalty within the people. Civil war broke out, and several of the members moved to the States to start a new life. They called their leader King, his wife Queen, his daughter—"

"Princess," I finished on a whisper.

And then all I saw was a burning fire.

A mansion with flames devouring it whole.

A gunshot.

He fell.

And then my mom throwing a blanket over my head, getting me into the car. Driving. We drove for so long. We flew even longer.

I shook my head. "So, this Sinacore family..."

"They've been searching for the rightful heir. You have millions upon millions in a trust only you can access. Houses, cars—once the war was over it was preserved for you, but your mother…" Nixon moved toward me. "She was afraid it was all a ruse, and by then she'd fallen in love again—only this time with one of our men who was sent to kill the last remaining heir. Only he couldn't. He couldn't kill you or your mother. He said he fell in love with you the minute he met you. And said he'd protect you both and spy for us in exchange for your lives."

I squeezed my eyes shut. "He died because he knew too much."

"He died because his job was finished," Tex piped up.

I stumbled into the wall, my mind racing. "Was Vic a ruse too? A distraction to get me to trust you guys?"

"No!" Vic roared from his spot on the floor.

"You're going to Sicily tonight." Nixon touched my shoulder. "The betrothal contract made between your biological father and the Sinacore family still exists—you have no choice. To break it would start a war we can't afford to engage in! The five families will not go to war with Sicily over one woman."

Each word he delivered was like a shot to my soul.

"No!" I yelled. "I won't do it! I don't love him! I can't…I can't be with him." I brought a shaky hand to my face as terror wrapped its talons around my throat and squeezed.

"Shhh." Luc pulled me into a hug but I shoved her away, I shoved her away and ran. I ran fast and hard. I ran into the backyard and stood under the tree. And then I ran the perimeter of the fence until I was far enough away that I could breathe.

The backyard had cameras everywhere, it wasn't like I could actually hide. I started to climb the rock wall that divided the garage and the tennis court, and caught my foot.

I grasped for a holding and twisted my ankle as I fell at an awkward angle onto the ground.

I had no choice.

I ran down the driveway, I limped and screamed. I cried until I couldn't see anymore.

And then I saw cars.

Four black sedans.

They looked nothing like the sports cars the rest of the family drove, and I had no place to hide.

So when one stopped, opened the door and someone said, "Get in."

I knew running would just injure me more.

I wiped my face and sat like the queen I was, with my back ramrod straight. The man looked to be about Vic's age. He grinned. "Andrei said to arrive early, and look how good fortune smiles down on us." The other three men in the car chuckled. "I think there has been a fruitful change of plans." He nodded to the driver. "Back to the club."

Chapter Twenty-Nine

Vic

"Let. Her. Go," Nixon snapped at me.

I stood to my full height and whispered, "Fucking make me."

His fist came down hard again. This time I shoved him away. He barely moved an inch because I didn't want a fight. I wanted to race after her, kiss her tears away, fall to my knees, and apologize.

"Could everyone just stop one damn second?" Tex lifted a gun in the air like he was ready to shoot it. "Whose brilliant idea was it to leave her alone with this one in the first place?" He pointed at me. Great.

So I smirked and pointed at Chase, who pointed at Nixon, you get the picture, hell of a lot of pointing.

"Oh, for shit's sake." Chase grabbed a knife out of his pocket and thumbed it. "Raise your hand if you think you could go without sex for more than a month let alone three years." Nobody raised their hands. "Exactly, and yet we ask him to do this, and guard her...you know he likes brown eyes!"

"The hell?" Phoenix narrowed his eyes at Chase. "So he throws all his hard work away?"

Dante snorted. "Every saint in this room throw the first punch, oh wait..." He glared at Nixon, "We asked the impossible...because we wanted him to protect the women, the children, our future... That's a hell of a lot to put on someone's shoulders. How is it fair to ask this of him? He guards our future but gets nothing but darkness in his? No children? No family?"

"Ah, wisdom from the youngest, that's rare." Tex piped up.

Dante gave him the finger while Sergio stared at his phone and then muttered a loud enough curse to gain everyone's attention.

"We have a problem." Sergio looked ready to shove his phone up someone's ass.

"We?" Nixon crossed his arms.

"Yes, *we*." Sergio tossed him the phone. "Grab your shit. Andrei says Angelo is on his way to the club—and he has Renee in his backseat."

I was a blur of movement as I grabbed my holster only to have Nixon jerk my elbow and pull me back. "No chance in hell. You're too distracted, you could get yourself killed."

"Thought you already wanted to kill me."

His nostrils flared. "You're too distracted."

"Stop. Making. Decisions. For me," I growled. "She's mine!"

He took a step back, his eyebrows shooting up in surprise before he shared a look with an amused Chase.

"You heard the man." Chase grinned. "She's his."

"God help anyone who gets in his way," Tex muttered under his breath while I shoved past everyone and ran toward my G-Wagon. God help them indeed.

Because I was going to kill them all.

Chapter Thirty

Renee

The club was dark. People were in red and black with masks covering most of their faces. I couldn't make out anything recognizable other than the smell of cigars and whiskey. Women were sprawled around velvet couches while men openly kissed down their necks, between their legs, only to grab another companion and do the same to them.

I shuddered as I was brought to a dance section and then taken up black stairs to a red velvet rope. It was pulled aside and then I was being shoved toward a white couch. I stumbled and sat.

"What's this?" a familiar voice asked.

"My betrothed." The man winked over at me. "But here's the thing…if she dies or suddenly disappears, it makes my life much easier."

"Ah." Andrei nodded and took a seat, clasping his hands together. "Yes, I remember, your entire inheritance is tied up in this neat little marriage."

"Yes." He clenched his teeth together. "And I think…I'd rather have my money."

Andrei's jaw flexed, but his eyes didn't flicker. I glanced down at his right leg as it tapped against the ground in rapid succession. "How may I be of service?"

The man grinned. "I imagine she could get a large sum…Italian royalty? Even if she's a whore—she's still worth at least, oh—" He looked me over, from head to toe. I'd never felt so dirty in my entire life. "Seven million."

Dollars?

I tried hiding my shock.

"She's used goods," Andrei said in a bored tone. "That kind of money only goes to the virgins. The Sheiks do not like knowing their women have been with others and the princes we cater to would slit my throat for it. I'm sorry but you're going to have to do better than that, Angelo."

I stared straight ahead as they bartered my worth right in front of me. As I heard the music pumping around me, the sexual sighs and moans that accompanied it.

He would come.

Right?

Vic would find me.

He would.

I had to believe it.

And then what? I'd be sold to this maniac again?

Is that all I was? A bargaining chip?

The more I thought about it, the more depressed I became... Vic had never had a say in what happened to me.

Why would he now?

"Two million cash," Andrei said thoughtfully. "Final offer."

"Cash?" Angelo spurted. "Tonight?"

"Sign her over and promise to never show your face again and yes, tonight you will have two million dollars in cash. We'll just say she was killed by the dirty Russians or better yet taken by the Borello cartel, easy you get two million plus your trust fund when you turn twenty-eight and no nasty little betrothal to a woman who's clearly...too ugly to be by your side."

I flinched at his words. At his tone. At the way he carelessly spat them out and wielded them like both sword and shield. Andrei was a dangerous man indeed.

"Done." He stood and held out his hand.

Andrei stared at the hand for a few seconds, sniffed, then motioned for someone to come over.

A man who looked extremely Italian and a lot like Sergio held out a black folder and then handed over a heavy looking pen.

"Sign here," Andrei said gruffly.

Angelo signed, grinning the entire time.

I slumped into myself, already covering up what I was afraid would be exposed too soon.

"Ax," Andrei nodded to the man with the black folder. "Take two guards with you." He smiled at Angelo. "This concludes our business. Ax will take you to the vault where you will get paid."

And then they were gone.

Andrei sat down next to me. He didn't so much as look at me as he asked. "Are you injured?"

My throat was so dry it was hard to speak. "Ankle, I fell."

"Did he injure you?" Still he wouldn't look at me. "I could shoot him for selling damaged goods and not being upfront about it."

"Only my pride," I managed to joke, earning his gaze for the first time. He was pretty. He was also younger than I'd originally suspected. In his early twenties maybe. With light hair and perfect skin. Like a fallen angel who hadn't gotten the memo that he could return to heaven.

"I see why he likes you." He stood and held out his hand. "Should I taste you first?" I recoiled. He leaned down and whispered. "Play along, he still has men here."

I grabbed his hand.

He squeezed it tight and led me through a crowd. My ankle throbbed as I leaned against him. His free hand caressed my ass and squeezed. I closed my eyes. This was just the beginning, wasn't it? Angelo was making his way out of a separate room when Andrei spun me around and slammed me against the nearest wall. His mouth was hot and controlled, he kept his eyes open, locked on me while his lips moved effortlessly across mine. Like the man had studied how to make a kiss look passionate when to the person he was kissing—It felt emotionless.

His eyes darkened as he heaved me into his arms and parted his lips. I didn't kiss him back at first, and then a sharp pinch in my ass had me yelping into his mouth as he flicked his tongue with mine. He tasted like spicy whiskey and spearmint.

And then he abruptly stopped, pulled away, grabbed my hand, and we kept walking. "Necessary evil."

I almost stumbled. "Kissing me was a necessary evil?"

He kept his eyes straight ahead. "I don't mix business with pleasure. Kissing is merely an exchange of currency."

"I don't understand."

"Someone like you wouldn't." We stopped in front of a solid metal door, and he slid a black and red card through a slot. It opened with a weird sucking noise. The room was freezing. My teeth started chattering immediately.

"I don't understand," I said between cold breaths.

"Everyone has a currency. Most women use their bodies to buy what they want...most men pay it. I deal with those people. I am not one of them. And neither are you." His voice lowered as a light flickered in the middle of the room. There was a stage fixed with ropes coming from the ceiling along with different sorts of shackles and handcuffs.

I stopped walking.

"Take off your shoes," he instructed.

I fumbled with my shoes and finally got them off, including the one trying to trap my swollen ankle.

He grabbed a black silk robe and handed it to me. "Take off your clothes."

"No."

He sighed in impatience. "In this, you must trust me."

I stared him down. He just tilted his head in that predatory animalistic way that made a person wonder if his soul was still in his body or just barely tethered there by mere force. His eyes were empty.

But he was all I had.

And I knew that he and the Italians had a deal.

I was out of choices, wasn't I? This was the only path to take.

"F-fine." I took off my clothes while he watched. He didn't seem the least bit affected by my nakedness, as if he'd seen so much of it, it no longer stirred anything in him.

He pointed up at the hazy ceiling. "Green light means you've been purchased. Red light means you'll be tortured. I would start praying for that green light...even Italians are bloodthirsty when it comes to torture—and I have no way of knowing if the ones who have a claim on you mean to let you live—or want to watch you suffer."

"Please!" I grabbed him by the arm. He stared down at my fingers like he wasn't used to human contact and then jerked away from me. I grasped at him again. "Please, don't leave me here."

His eyes softened. "If it makes you feel better, I'm seventy percent sure you'll see a green light, and if you see red, I'll shoot you before the pain becomes unbearable. Agreed?"

Tears streamed down my face. He shoved a handkerchief into my hands as his footsteps echoed across the cement floor.

Why cement?

And why out of all the things I would be thinking about would that be something that entered my head? The club was beautiful, no expense was spared, and cement? I stared after him as the door locked shut.

The lights flickered on all around me.

Drains were placed every few feet within the cement.

And lining the wall were chains like you'd see in a dungeon. Blood stained a few of them, and in one of them was a woman, eyes open, mouth slack. I opened my mouth to scream when the panel she was connected to was sucked back into the wall. A red curtain replaced the area like nothing had ever happened.

I'd wrongly assumed it was some sort of naughty playground.

No, that's not what this was.

This was…the pit of hell.

The main stage looked like something out of a horror movie. What was worse? There seemed to be places to sit in the back, lavish couches like they had in the VIP section with buckets of champagne in the middle of each of the tables.

What sort of man was Andrei? To let this happen? To bank on this?

If kissing and sex wasn't his currency, did that mean torture was?

I wrapped my arms around my middle and slowly walked toward the stage and sat at the edge. My eyes locked on the lights above.

"Please, Vic. Please find me."

Chapter Thirty-One

Vic

I didn't remember driving to the club. My rage was fueled by three things. Find her. Keep her safe. Kill anyone in my way.

I jumped out of my SUV, a Glock in each hand.

"Vic," Nixon called after me.

I stopped in my tracks. Too pissed to turn around and face him.

"This won't end the way you want it to," he said in a clear voice.

"I took a punishment. Don't let her be punished for my actions further, Nixon. I have a plan."

I could sense his hesitation.

Sense the bosses as they looked at one another.

Chase took a step forward. "We've trusted you for three years."

I finally turned to see all of them heavily armed, staring at Nixon. Waiting. Tex didn't step in because it was family business—and I was owned by the Abandonatos.

"If you can find a way to fix this," Nixon said in a low voice, "fix it. But nothing can trace back to us, back to her. Fuck this up and I kill you. No hesitation. No mistakes."

I nodded. "Thank you."

"We've got your back, Vic." Nixon cocked his gun and shook his head. "Just had to fall for the nanny."

"Told ya, brown eyes." Dante smirked.

We walked in solidarity toward the black door. I knocked twice just as the door swung open. "Move."

The bodyguard widened his eyes as he stared down the barrel of the gun in my right hand.

With a sigh he shook his head. "One gun per person."

"Tough shit, I have seven. Move."

"Vic—" The guy cursed in Russian. "I can't, you know I can't."

"You can," I said with a smug grin. "You will."

He knew I wasn't bluffing. He knew my madness; it was etched all over my face. I would kill him in cold blood even though I knew he had a family, even though I knew he had a kid on the way. I wouldn't blink.

He knew.

So I gave him three seconds.

When I should have given him nothing.

He wiped his hands down his face. "At least hit me so it looks like there was a struggle."

"No problem." I knocked him out with my gun and stormed through the front door. The loud music was already giving me a headache as I ran down the first main hall and into the dance area. Andrei yet again was looking over his kingdom. He sighed when he saw me, and then grinned when the rest of the bosses filed in after me.

The music kept going, but people obviously took notice that a shit ton of giant Italians had just walked into what was notoriously known as a Russian-run club. A Russian-run club that catered to all sorts of lifestyles and backgrounds—a club that loved torturing Italian girls and selling them on the streets.

Andrei nodded to me.

I made my way up the stairs, my guns at my sides as he took a seat at his usual couch and spread his arms across the back off the chair. "Are you here for the girl?"

"What did you do?" I pointed both guns at his face.

It was the first time I'd seen the guy full-on grin. "You're welcome."

"What the fuck?" I roared.

He just shrugged while the rest of the guys filed in next to me.

Tex was the next to speak. "Did you decorate or were you able to find a vampire who was willing to do it for half price?"

Andrei shot him a look of disgust. "Werewolf, actually."

"Where is she?" I said again, and this time my voice shook with so much anger I was having a hard time not shooting him just to shoot him.

He sighed like he was bored, then stood. "Follow me."

We walked toward the direction of The Cage.

No. He wouldn't put her in there.

He wouldn't.

My fingers itched to pull both triggers.

"Remember…" Andrei sighed. "I'm your ally."

"I might question that if you put her on the block, you sick fuck!" I roared.

He rolled his eyes. "Calm down. Plus, what did you want me to do? Just hand her over after a two million dollar transaction?"

Nixon put his hand on Andrei's chest. "Explain. Now."

"Angelo's a little prick who wants access to his trust fund. Everything was tied into this marriage…but if she's sold and he goes back and has proof of her death then…what's a father to do but give his son all his money?"

"What?" I shook my head.

"I gave him two million dollars for the honor of torturing her."

I lunged but Tex and Phoenix held me back.

"Now…" Andrei led us onto the balcony overlooking the main stage. She was shivering on the side, hugging her body while people around her started poking and prodding her like she was some sort of object they could purchase. "Here is your button. Just type in the number of the girl you want to pay for…and press the light for what sort of activity you'd like to embark on. Might I suggest the hanging tower of death? Best orgasm of some men's lives."

I pointed the gun at his head. "Release her."

Andrei spread his arms wide. "I'm a business man, remember? This is where I've been placed. I can't hand her over. But you can purchase her. The way everyone else has to purchase in this establishment. My suggestion would be to hurry, since several men have already asked her price and I can't keep lying and saying twelve million especially when one of them actually contemplated it…" He shoved his hands in his pockets. "Two million. And no matter what choice you make with the light—no judgment, Vic—she'll be pronounced dead, which means that either she goes under your protection, or hell's."

The sleek flat device felt cold in my hand as he shoved it toward me and then left me staring down at her.

"I could just kill them all," I whispered.

"Would it make you feel better if you did?" Nixon asked.

"Yes."

He sighed. "It would be unwise to create an even bigger mess when Andrei's this deep in... Just...buy her and be done with it."

"Be done with it!" I shoved against his chest. "I love her!"

"THEN BUY HER!" he roared back.

It wasn't that.

I could buy her seven times over.

It was that I was buying her.

And then letting her go.

And I didn't want to let her go.

I wanted to buy her and run away with her. I wanted to buy her and marry her. I wanted to buy her and let her go to school wherever she wanted, finish her degree. I wanted her freedom.

With shaking hands I pressed the number dangling above her head where she sat....and then hit the red button.

Chapter Thirty-Two

Renee

I shivered as the screen flashed with the number above my head…And then the light went red. I gaped at it like it wasn't true. It couldn't be true. Not only had he not come in time, but I was going to be tortured to death.

Though Andrei did promise he'd kill me.

This wasn't happening.

How was it real?

I stood on shaky feet as two men walked into the room, made a beeline toward me, then jerked me toward a door on the opposite side. They shoved me through it and closed the door behind them.

The room was pitch-black except for a small dim chandelier that hung over a red satin bed. There were no windows.

Just satin and velvet everywhere I looked, and several different drawers and closets that probably held weapons that would haunt me even in my death.

Movement behind me caught my eye as I ran toward the bed and tried to hide on one side of it.

Then footsteps.

Someone was coming out of the shadows.

I closed my eyes.

It would be over soon. It would all be over.

"I was watching you," came the familiar voice. "And I realized once again that if all I was allowed in this life—was the honor of watching you, I would take it."

"Vic?" I asked, as hope filled my chest. "Please tell me this isn't a trick."

"No trick." He moved around the bed and leaned down. He had four different guns strapped to his chest, more probably on his back, and looked ready to start an all-out war.

"But how?" I reached for him, then pulled away in shame.

He tilted my chin toward him. "I'll always find you, Renee. Always."

"I didn't mean to run, I was just so upset, I'm still upset, I can't trust anyone, I can't—"

He silenced me with a kiss then pulled away. "You can trust me. I would have told you everything had it not put your life in danger, and mine. We were already pushing too many lines. One more would have..." He sighed. "I guess it doesn't matter anymore, does it?"

I frowned. "What do you mean, it doesn't matter?"

"I love you." He kissed my forehead. "Never forget that, all right?"

"But..."

He stood and pulled out one of his guns.

"No, Vic! No!"

"Trust me," he said softly. "Trust me to take care of you."

"You're pointing a gun at me!" I snapped. "How can I trust that?"

"You know me, Renee. You know the real me. Trust me in this...please. It's the only way."

"Killing me is the only way?"

"I never said I was going to kill you," he said in a lethal voice.

I frowned just as the first gunshot rang out. It hit the pillow next to my head. I screamed and covered myself with my hands. More shots followed until all I heard were gunshots.

And then the door was opening behind him and what looked like a strung-out woman was thrown onto the bed.

Andrei cracked his neck. "She's the closest I could find...and she is of no use to us anymore."

She started laughing loudly and taking off her clothes. She looked near death as bullet holes decorated her thin legs along with cigarette burns. Her arms were slashed up like she'd been cutting herself in order to escape her hell, and she was so high she started shrieking about demons on her face.

Vic shot her without taking his eyes off me.

I watched him while he put bullets into her body.

When all the blood was spilled, and mixed with down feathers and red satin from the bed, Vic snapped his fingers as Andrei handed him something black.

"Trust me," he said just before pulling it over my head and throwing me over his shoulder.

"That was fun!" Andrei laughed smugly. "Come back soon!"

I wanted to give him all the middle fingers, mixed with all the tears. I wanted to scream and rage and pound my fists into Vic's back. That is until I felt the cold night air against my legs.

And then a door was opening.

Familiar voices sounded.

"Any clean up?" Dante.

"No," Vic said harshly.

"Damn." Chase.

"She's probably in shock." Tex.

"Who wouldn't be in shock?" Sergio.

"Take her back to the house." Nixon.

"Looks like I have a new black folder on yet another family member... You see how the world works? We give and we give, and it gives right back. I'll enjoy this one immensely, I think." Phoenix.

They kept talking like it wasn't a big deal that some random woman was dead in that room, or that their friend Andrei was dealing with whatever horrors he was dealing in.

Vic heaved me into the leather back seat tossed the keys to Phoenix. And scooted in next to me as the vehicle drove off.

I shook in his arms.

He never let me go.

And when we finally stopped.

And I was getting carried into the familiar smell of Nixon's house— they pulled the black hood from my head, and I collapsed against Vic's chest. Gut-wrenching sobs came from my lips as I clawed for him, scrambled for his embrace.

He gave it. He held me tight.

And I hated them.

I hated all of them.

I hated the life.

And I hated the necessity of what had just happened.

That someone had to die so I could live.

"We'll talk later," Nixon whispered. "Good work tonight. I

wouldn't have thought that clearly... I would have pressed the green button and exposed everyone and everything—because when you love someone all you can focus on is getting them to safety. You proved something extraordinary tonight, Vic. I hope you know that."

Vic nodded to him and carried me down the hall toward his bedroom.

Once inside, he shut the door behind him and set me on my feet. I lunged. I hit him with my fists until I couldn't feel my hands anymore, and when I yelled at him, he let me until I stopped hitting him, until I lost all energy—until I beat the fear out of myself.

"It's okay." Vic cupped my face, wiping my tears away with his thumbs. "You're safe now, it's going to be okay."

"It's not!" I choked on a sob. "Nixon's going to send me back to Angelo or or or—"

"You're dead," Vic said in a quiet voice. "You belong to no one but yourself."

"But—" I sniffed. "What about you? Why can't I belong to you?"

His lips twitched and then he full on smiled. "I never said you couldn't."

"But the oath—"

"Fuck the oath." He pulled me against his chest. "I live for you now."

Chapter Thirty-Three

Vic

Her eyes lit up as more tears fell down her face. "Me?"

"Give me the choice, Renee, them or you, and it will be you every single time. Tell me to walk away and I will."

"You would walk away from this life?"

"This isn't living," I said sadly. "I want a life with you. Only you."

"But what about your family? You can't just leave them…"

"I'm replaceable." I shrugged.

She glared like she knew it wasn't true.

With a sigh I pulled her tight against my chest. "I don't want stolen moments with you anymore. I want slow…I want your body sweaty in my hands while I make love to you—I want to drive you crazy with my tongue, to make you wild with each touch. No more rushing things between us, Renee. Not anymore. Because I'm yours."

"No." She shook her head.

My heart stopped beating in that no. "What?"

"I can't be yours unless you give me your word."

"On what?"

"Give it to me first."

I pulled away and crossed my arms. "That's not typically how these things work."

She smiled. "I know. But I know how stubborn you are. Your word, please." Of course I could see the outline of her breasts and was distracted as hell with the need to just be inside her and make sure she was okay.

"You have my word."

"Great." She grabbed my hand and stomped out of the room with me in tow. We stopped once she made it into the loud kitchen— naturally there was wine everywhere and angry talk about not getting to shoot anything.

"Nixon." She barked out his name like she had a right to.

Nixon's expression couldn't be any more stunned.

"What you did, keeping that from me was wrong." She lifted her chin in the air like the royalty she was. "Is it true though? If there was a sort of rank in here...would I be more important than say even...Tex?"

"Watch it." Tex stood then winked at her.

Nixon grinned. "Yeah, probably."

"Hey!" Tex looked actually hurt.

"What's on your mind?" Nixon seemed extremely amused.

"Well, I have demands."

"Nannies don't get demands."

"Princess," she corrected. "Right?"

Nixon full-on laughed. "Yeah, all right, your highness, what are your demands?"

"Him." She pulled me forward. "Just him."

The guys stared at me with such shit-eating grins I wanted to shoot every one of them.

Chase just leaned back in his chair with a shrewd smile like he'd known it would turn out this way. Yeah, right.

"Anything else?" Nixon frowned.

"And..." She gulped. "I want to cook for family dinner at least once a month."

"No!" Chase roared. "She'll ruin it!"

"Sit down." Dante jerked him by the shirt.

"Family dinners, huh? Does that mean you're sticking around?" Nixon walked toward her. "I do have a guest house, multiple rooms...but by the look in my cousin's eyes—" He wasn't even looking at me, the bastard could probably just smell the arousal from there. "— I'd maybe aim for more privacy..."

I gave him the finger.

Everyone burst out laughing.

"No time for that." She smiled sweetly. "So I suggest you wear ear plugs tonight, big guy...it's going to be a fun few hours. After all, I did just get rescued and apparently I'm worth more than you are."

I choked on a laugh.

"That's fair." Nixon chuckled and then held out his hand. "Are we shaking on this?"

"Blood oath." She lifted her chin into the air again.

Damn it. The woman was going to cut herself over this? Over me?

"You've been paying better attention than I thought," Nixon muttered as he took out his knife and sliced down the middle of his hand then grabbed hers and did the same, much lighter. He pressed his palm to hers. "I swear on my life that Vic is released from his oath, that he's yours in every way—that you're his—" She cleared her throat. "—and," expression weary, he added, "that you can cook family dinner at least once a month."

"Son of a bitch," Chase muttered from his spot at the table.

Renee sighed, pulled her hand away, then leaned up and kissed Nixon on both cheeks. "Thank you."

"My pleasure," he said in a serious tone as he held her gaze.

"Just had to fall for the nanny…" Tex piped up.

"Bet she'll kiss his boo boos and make him the best mac and cheese—"

That comment earned a slap from someone, and then knives were pulled, and guns. Wine was spilled.

It was a typical day in the life. I didn't respond, just grabbed the med kit and pulled out some antiseptic and started working on Renee's hand amidst the continuation of everyone drinking. When I was finished I squeezed her hand and led her back down the hall.

The minute we were in my room, I slammed the door shut.

And didn't lock it.

Let them see.

Let them see who I loved.

Who I would die for.

Who I'd made an oath to live for.

"I love you," she whispered between kisses as she pushed me against the door, stretching her soft body against mine. "Thank you for saving my life."

"It's you—" I pulled back and looked into her eyes. "—who saved mine."

Our mouths collided. I pulled back and laughed. I laughed hard because I was happy. Because she made me happy.

Because for the first time in a long time—I knew joy.

And when I tossed her onto the bed and kissed every inch of skin, when I tasted her body, when I thrust into her slow and smooth and let myself feel the rhythm of her body…

I swore that I would do everything in my power to make sure she was never hurt or threatened again.

I rose over her, my breathing ragged. "You're my joy."

Her eyes lit up as she wrapped her arms around my neck and moved her hips against me. I coaxed a slow burning fire between us, ripples of pleasure sending shock waves through both of our bodies.

Nobody would ever love her the way I loved her.

"Vic." She locked eyes with me. "My Vic."

Epilogue

He was watching me again.

I could feel it in my body, in the way I burned for him, from my fingers all the way down to my toes. I licked my lips in anticipation and tried to focus on the conversation with my mom.

"Those were dangerous times," she said with such heavy sadness that I was convinced if I reached into the thin air I could grab it, stare at it, taste it, and see every single mental picture she had painted and feel pain all over again. "But your father, your biological father," she corrected. "He sacrificed his life for us."

I reached for her hand and squeezed. "Did he suffer?"

I felt the room pause as eyes fell to me, as the people standing around acting casual after our wedding showed their true colors. Eavesdropping. Maybe they paused, maybe they reacted because they knew the truth.

In the mafia there would always be suffering.

It came hand in hand with finding true love.

It was a sacrifice we were all willing to make—to find the one that made our heart beat when we faced death on a daily basis.

"No." She smiled down at our joined hands, at the small brown photo album with its five pictures and torn plastic pages. "Where there is love—suffering cannot exist, only love. Love casts out all fear where suffering resides, there is only determination, protection, there is only sacrifice. That is what love truly is, dying to yourself regardless of the cost."

I didn't realize I was crying until my mom released my hand and touched my cheeks with both of hers. "Your biological father loved you as much as the father you knew. Both saved us just in different ways. And now—" She looked over my shoulder. "Now you have found a man willing to do anything to keep you safe. In our world, that bravery runs deeper than love. It is life. And he is willing to give his, for yours."

She kissed me on the cheek and stood, walking off toward the kitchen like the air wasn't heavy with her words. Like I wasn't still staring at the pictures in my hand.

I swallowed the ball in my throat and looked up. Vic had snuck up on me, again.

Surprise, surprise.

He was way too talented at making no noise. Sometimes I asked him if he practiced not breathing.

He said he was just skilled.

Right.

Skilled at silence.

"What are you doing?" I tilted my head and set the small plastic album down on the couch.

He just smirked, in fact his smirk grew into a full-blown smile as he knelt down and grabbed my hands, then whispered gruffly against my neck, "What I do best." I sucked in a breath. "I'm watching the nanny."

"Like what you see?" I bit down on my lower lip.

"Love it." He pulled back and cupped my face then pressed a gentle kiss to the corner of my mouth. "Love you."

"I love you too."

He stood and pulled me to my feet, then jerked me against his chest. "Guess you're just going to have to prove it again."

I didn't miss the sly wink Chase sent our way as we casually walked to the hall bathroom, just like I didn't miss Andrei's blank expression as if he wasn't even in the room with us.

But somewhere far away.

Somewhere dead.

And my gut clenched even tighter because I knew—unless you had light to balance out the dark—you would not survive.

Not in this life.

"He's fine," Vic said, closing the door behind us, pushing me against it. "Some of us feed off the darkness—so I say let him feed, let it grow, until it gets so big he has to fight it himself."

"The monster?"

"He is the monster. We all are. Let it get big enough to where he has to make a choice…"

"What's that?"

"Fight or succumb."

"You fought."

He brushed a kiss across my lips. "You gave me a reason to."

I gripped his biceps and held us there. In that moment, I could have sworn I felt the beat of his heart as it sang my name as my heart joined its cadence.

Forever. I was his forever.

Until death do us part.

Or until this cruel world rips us from each other.

I was his.

He was mine.

"I watch you too." I whispered. "Every day."

"I know." He grinned. "I've always known…it's the first thing I noticed about you, your intense stare… I found love in that stare. I knew the only way to get your attention…was to stare right back."

"I love you," I said through streaming tears.

He just grinned and repeated what he'd said before. "Prove it."

* * * *

Also from 1001 Dark Nights and Rachel Van Dyken, discover Abandon and All Stars Fall.

* * * *

Want more Einstein?

Check out New York Times bestselling author Molly McAdam's Rebel Series!

http://smarturl.it/McAdamsAmazon

Our Eagle Elite/Rebel crossover takes place in Molly McAdam's *Lock*!

http://smarturl.it/LockAmazon

Sign up for the 1001 Dark Nights Newsletter
and be entered to win a Tiffany Key necklace.

There's a contest every month!

Go to www.1001DarkNights.com to subscribe.

**As a bonus, all subscribers can download
FIVE FREE exclusive books!**

Discover 1001 Dark Nights Collection Six

Go to www.1001DarkNights.com for more information.

DRAGON CLAIMED by Donna Grant
A Dark Kings Novella

ASHES TO INK by Carrie Ann Ryan
A Montgomery Ink: Colorado Springs Novella

ENSNARED by Elisabeth Naughton
An Eternal Guardians Novella

EVERMORE by Corinne Michaels
A Salvation Series Novella

VENGEANCE by Rebecca Zanetti
A Dark Protectors/Rebels Novella

ELI'S TRIUMPH by Joanna Wylde
A Reapers MC Novella

CIPHER by Larissa Ione
A Demonica Underworld Novella

RESCUING MACIE by Susan Stoker
A Delta Force Heroes Novella

ENCHANTED by Lexi Blake
A Masters and Mercenaries Novella

TAKE THE BRIDE by Carly Phillips
A Knight Brothers Novella

INDULGE ME by J. Kenner
A Stark Ever After Novella

THE KING by Jennifer L. Armentrout
A Wicked Novella

QUIET MAN by Kristen Ashley
A Dream Man Novella

ABANDON by Rachel Van Dyken
A Seaside Pictures Novella

THE OPEN DOOR by Laurelin Paige
A Found Duet Novella

CLOSER by Kylie Scott
A Stage Dive Novella

SOMETHING JUST LIKE THIS by Jennifer Probst
A Stay Novella

BLOOD NIGHT by Heather Graham
A Krewe of Hunters Novella

TWIST OF FATE by Jill Shalvis
A Heartbreaker Bay Novella

MORE THAN PLEASURE YOU by Shayla Black
A More Than Words Novella

WONDER WITH ME by Kristen Proby
A With Me In Seattle Novella

THE DARKEST ASSASSIN by Gena Showalter
A Lords of the Underworld Novella

Also from 1001 Dark Nights:
DAMIEN by J. Kenner

Discover 1001 Dark Nights

Go to www.1001DarkNights.com for more information.

COLLECTION ONE
FOREVER WICKED by Shayla Black
CRIMSON TWILIGHT by Heather Graham
CAPTURED IN SURRENDER by Liliana Hart
SILENT BITE: A SCANGUARDS WEDDING by Tina Folsom
DUNGEON GAMES by Lexi Blake
AZAGOTH by Larissa Ione
NEED YOU NOW by Lisa Renee Jones
SHOW ME, BABY by Cherise Sinclair
ROPED IN by Lorelei James
TEMPTED BY MIDNIGHT by Lara Adrian
THE FLAME by Christopher Rice
CARESS OF DARKNESS by Julie Kenner

COLLECTION TWO
WICKED WOLF by Carrie Ann Ryan
WHEN IRISH EYES ARE HAUNTING by Heather Graham
EASY WITH YOU by Kristen Proby
MASTER OF FREEDOM by Cherise Sinclair
CARESS OF PLEASURE by Julie Kenner
ADORED by Lexi Blake
HADES by Larissa Ione
RAVAGED by Elisabeth Naughton
DREAM OF YOU by Jennifer L. Armentrout
STRIPPED DOWN by Lorelei James
RAGE/KILLIAN by Alexandra Ivy/Laura Wright
DRAGON KING by Donna Grant
PURE WICKED by Shayla Black
HARD AS STEEL by Laura Kaye
STROKE OF MIDNIGHT by Lara Adrian
ALL HALLOWS EVE by Heather Graham
KISS THE FLAME by Christopher Rice
DARING HER LOVE by Melissa Foster
TEASED by Rebecca Zanetti
THE PROMISE OF SURRENDER by Liliana Hart

COLLECTION THREE
HIDDEN INK by Carrie Ann Ryan
BLOOD ON THE BAYOU by Heather Graham
SEARCHING FOR MINE by Jennifer Probst
DANCE OF DESIRE by Christopher Rice
ROUGH RHYTHM by Tessa Bailey
DEVOTED by Lexi Blake
Z by Larissa Ione
FALLING UNDER YOU by Laurelin Paige
EASY FOR KEEPS by Kristen Proby
UNCHAINED by Elisabeth Naughton
HARD TO SERVE by Laura Kaye
DRAGON FEVER by Donna Grant
KAYDEN/SIMON by Alexandra Ivy/Laura Wright
STRUNG UP by Lorelei James
MIDNIGHT UNTAMED by Lara Adrian
TRICKED by Rebecca Zanetti
DIRTY WICKED by Shayla Black
THE ONLY ONE by Lauren Blakely
SWEET SURRENDER by Liliana Hart

COLLECTION FOUR
ROCK CHICK REAWAKENING by Kristen Ashley
ADORING INK by Carrie Ann Ryan
SWEET RIVALRY by K. Bromberg
SHADE'S LADY by Joanna Wylde
RAZR by Larissa Ione
ARRANGED by Lexi Blake
TANGLED by Rebecca Zanetti
HOLD ME by J. Kenner
SOMEHOW, SOME WAY by Jennifer Probst
TOO CLOSE TO CALL by Tessa Bailey
HUNTED by Elisabeth Naughton
EYES ON YOU by Laura Kaye
BLADE by Alexandra Ivy/Laura Wright
DRAGON BURN by Donna Grant
TRIPPED OUT by Lorelei James
STUD FINDER by Lauren Blakely
MIDNIGHT UNLEASHED by Lara Adrian

Discover More Rachel Van Dyken

Abandon: A Seaside Pictures Novella
By Rachel Van Dyken

Coming August 27, 2019

It's not every day you're slapped on stage by two different women you've been dating for the last year.

I know what you're thinking. What sort of ballsy woman gets on stage and slaps a rockstar? Does nobody have self-control anymore? It may have been the talk of the Grammy's.

Oh, yeah, forgot to mention that. I, Ty Cuban, was taken down by two psychotic women in front of the entire world. Lucky for us the audience thought it was part of the breakup song my band and I had just finished performing. I was thirty-three, hardly ready to settle down.

Except now it's getting forced on me. Seaside, Oregon. My band mates were more than happy to settle down, dig their roots into the sand, and start popping out kids. Meanwhile I was still enjoying life.

Until now. Until my forced hiatus teaching freaking guitar lessons at the local studio for the next two months. Part of my punishment, do something for the community while I think deep thoughts about all my life choices.

Sixty days of hell.

It doesn't help that the other volunteer is a past flame that literally looks at me as if I've sold my soul to the devil. She has the voice of an angel and looks to kill—I would know, because she looks ready to kill me every second of every day. I broke her heart when we were on tour together a decade ago.

I'm ready to put the past behind us. She's ready to run me over with her car then stand on top of it and strum her guitar with glee.

Sixty days. I can do anything for sixty days. Including making the sexy Von Abigail fall for me all over again. This time for good.

Damn, maybe there's something in the water.

* * * *

All Stars Fall: A Seaside Pictures/Big Sky Novella
By Rachel Van Dyken

She *left*.
Two words I can't really get out of my head.
She left *us*.
Three more words that make it that much worse.
Three being another word I can't seem to wrap my mind around.
Three kids under the age of six, and she left because she missed it. Because her dream had never been to have a family, no her dream had been to marry a rockstar and live the high life.

Moving my recording studio to Seaside Oregon seems like the best idea in the world right now especially since Seaside Oregon has turned into the place for celebrities to stay and raise families in between touring and producing. It would be lucrative to make the move, but I'm doing it for my kids because they need normal, they deserve normal. And me? Well, I just need a break and help, that too. I need a sitter and fast. Someone who won't flip me off when I ask them to sign an Iron Clad NDA, someone who won't sell our pictures to the press, and most of all? Someone who looks absolutely nothing like my ex-wife.

He's tall.
That was my first instinct when I saw the notorious Trevor Wood, drummer for the rock band Adrenaline, in the local coffee shop. He ordered a tall black coffee which made me smirk, and five minutes later I somehow agreed to interview for a nanny position. I couldn't help it; the smaller one had gum stuck in her hair while the eldest was standing on his feet and asking where babies came from. He looked so pathetic, so damn sexy and pathetic that rather than be star-struck, I took pity. I knew though; I knew the minute I signed that NDA, the minute our fingers brushed and my body became insanely aware of how close he was—I was in dangerous territory, I just didn't know how dangerous until it was too late. Until I fell for the star and realized that no matter how high they are in the sky—they're still human and fall just as hard.

About Rachel Van Dyken

Rachel Van Dyken is the New York Times, Wall Street Journal, and USA Today Bestselling author of regency and contemporary romances. When she's not writing you can find her drinking coffee at Starbucks and plotting her next book while watching The Bachelor.

She keeps her home in Idaho with her husband, adorable son, and two snoring boxers! She loves to hear from readers!

Want to be kept up to date on new releases? Text MAFIA to 66866!

You can connect with her on Facebook:
www.facebook.com/rachelvandyken
or join her fan group Rachel's New Rockin Readers.
Her website is www.rachelvandykenauthor.com.

Elicit
Eagle Elite Book 4
By Rachel Van Dyken
Now Available

Hey readers! I hope you enjoyed Envy! If you want to dive into the series where things start getting gritty and oh so sexy, I always personally recommend readers start with Elicit! The first few books have a very YA feel to them and since I started the series in a college location, some readers prefer to start where you get all the hot tension and all the sexy times!

* * * *

Cursed, numb, rejected, scorned, wicked, sinister, dark, twisted...my name is Tex Campisi and this is my legacy. I killed my father in cold blood and lost my soul right along with him.

I crave war more than peace, and I'm about to take my place in history as the youngest Capo dei Capi in the Cosa Nostra...that is until someone stops me, saves me from myself.

But the only person able to do that...is my best friends sister, Mo Abandonato, and she just ripped my heart out and asked me to hold it in my hands while she put bullets through it.

Im cursed so I did it.

I'm numb so I held it.

I'm wicked so I liked it.

I used the pain Mo caused as a catalyst to turn into my biggest nightmare--the five families greatest enemy. It's my turn to take a stand, knowing full well I'm going to lose my mind to the madness that is the American Mafia. I've always been told Blood is thicker than life. I wish I would have listened. Because regardless of who you love? You will betray. You will kill.

Blood Always Wins.

The only way out is death...yours.

Welcome to the Dark Side of the Family.

* * * *

"Eight minutes where I'd rather time didn't exist." I whispered watching pain roll across his face in a wave. "Kiss me again."

With a soft exhale, he brushed his lips across mine, little feathery strokes that tempted me with promises of something more. He used his tongue to trace the outline of my lips before sliding inside, past my teeth, tasting every inch of me, giving me every inch he could of himself. Living in the moment, both of us knowing that it would soon be over.

"Seven." I whispered against his mouth.

"Go to school," he urged for a second time. "Make mistakes, Mo. Get in trouble, let Nixon find you sneaking wine into your backpack. Get sent to the Dean's office, make mistakes," he said again then licked his lips. "Let someone pick up the pieces of your broken heart, let someone fix what I destroyed."

"What if I want to drop out and hermit myself in my room?" I refused to look at him.

"That's not living, Mo." Tex cupped my face. "I have five minutes left with you, do you want me to use it to kiss you or lecture you on why I'm right?"

I grinned as a tear slid down my cheek. "Both."

His smile matched mine. "I forget how much you like being scolded."

"Only if the one scolding has a firm hand."

"Every last inch of me is firm and you know it." Tex tugged me into his lap. "School will distract you, it will give you a better future then guns and war, it will take your focus from tragedy to the future. Please, for me, Mo, please try to do normal."

"Normal." I shook my head. "Not sure I know what that word is."

"Normal," Tex repeated. "Making love to someone under a tree not because you have to say goodbye, but because it's the best way you can think to say hello."

My lower lip quivered.

"Normal." His voice was hoarse. "Marrying the love of your life not because her brother shoots you at point blank range--but because not marrying her would be a fate worse than death."

He was silent then added, "Three minutes."

I clenched his shirt with my hands and fought the urge to sob against his chest.

"Normal." Tex's voice was barely audible. "Going from country to country, traveling all over the world, not because you have a hit on you, but because you want to see the girl you love smile in every country God ever created."

I knew the time was ticking by, it seemed the less time we had the faster it went, I guess that's life.

I was looking at two more minutes, maybe less, with my lover, my friend, and all I could do was clench his shirt in my hands and twist, somehow willing him to stay on the ground rather than get up and walk towards certain death.

"Normal." Tex moved to his feet, helping me up. "Giving the woman you love two hours of your time, because you can't imagine spending your minutes, those precious seconds, any other way."

Tex kissed my mouth hard, nearly bruising my lips before stepping back and kissing my nose.

"Time's up," he said gruffly.

"We're no longer friends." I said it as a statement, not even a question.

"For two hours I was your lover, your friend, your everything." Tex looked away. "For the rest of eternity--I'm now your enemy."

Elite
Eagle Elite Book 1
By Rachel Van Dyken

And if you want to start back at the beginning (my personal favorite even though it reads very New Adult) you can start with Elite, where Trace is just about to get dropped off at Eagle Elite University and Nixon? Well he's on the prowl...

* * * *

For Tracey Rooks, life with her grandparents on a Wyoming farm has always been simple. But after her grandmother's death, Tracey is all her grandfather has. So when Eagle Elite University announces its annual scholarship lottery, Tracey jumps at the opportunity to secure their future and enters. She isn't expecting much-but then she wins. And life as she knows it will never be same...

The students at Eagle Elite are unlike any she's ever met...and they refuse to make things easy for her. There's Nixon, gorgeous, irresistible, and leader of a group that everyone fears: The Elect. Their rules are simple. 1. Do not touch The Elect. 2. Do not look at The Elect. 3. Do not speak to The Elect. No matter how hard she tries to stay away, The Elect are always around her and it isn't long until she finds out the reason why they keep their friends close and their enemies even closer. She just didn't realize she was the enemy—until it was too late.

On behalf of 1001 Dark Nights,

Liz Berry and M.J. Rose would like to thank ~

Steve Berry
Doug Scofield
Kim Guidroz
Jillian Stein
InkSlinger PR
Dan Slater
Asha Hossain
Chris Graham
Fedora Chen
Kasi Alexander
Jessica Johns
Dylan Stockton
Richard Blake
and Simon Lipskar

Made in the USA
Lexington, KY
23 June 2019